KEN LANSDOWNE

SECRETS
DON'T
BELONG IN
CLOSETS

1

H Publishing
Denver, Colorado

Acknowledgements:

Many thanks to these people for their valuable help:
Kate Barefield and Edward Johnson for copyediting.
Also to Gayle Stevens, as well as Marty Kass, Andy
Thomas, Tammy Grossman, Steve Milk, & CW Davis.
To Stacy Mandell for her unflagging support and to Billy
Tipton, whose life was an inspiration.

Dedicated To:

HANS
Who always wanted to write
but didn't get to it before it
was to late.

Published by H Publishing
605 S. Clinton Street
Denver, Colorado 80247

Library of Congress Cataloging in Publication Data
Secrets don't belong in closets: a novel/ Ken Lansdowne
    p. cm.
  ISBN 0-9740853-2-4/978-0-9740853-2-6
  1. Title

Printed in USA   H Publishing

SECRETS
DON'T
BELONG IN
CLOSETS

Prologue

The man sat up. Then quickly grabbed his head to keep the tender brain inside from whacking against the sides of his skull. He moaned and thickly formed the words "Oh, God."

Running his fuzzy tongue across his equally fuzzy teeth left an after taste of old combat boot. That's not a bad thing if the guy who owned them was lying beside him. He checked. He wasn't.

His first rational thought, between throbs, was, What did I do last night? He came up blank. No answer. Nada. Nothing.

His stomach did a flip and he tasted the acid-ity remnants of last night's too many cigarettes and way too much alcohol. He stood, groaned, and sat back down. His sodden brain put together the fact he needed four things badly, all of which required his immediate presence in the bathroom. Standing, this time slowly, he padded on bare feet toward his goal.

Without turning on the hurtful light, he leaned his head against the tile above the toilet, fumbled at his groin, and completed the first of his require-ments.

Reaching to the medicine cabinet for the second, he noticed that his feet were sticking to the floor. Oh God, did I miss the bowl again last night?

He turned on the light and his head started to throb harder. Then harder as a keening wail forced its way onto his consciousness.

The wail was his.

He was screaming at the blood splattered on the walls, the floor, everywhere...

J eremy Bent, JB to those who knew him well, was in his usual position at nine A.M. on a Sunday morning. Fast asleep. But the ringing of the telephone was threatening to alter that state.

As a working writer JB tended to work until four or five in the morning and then sleep through the day. Most of the people who knew him knew this. Most of the people who knew him would never call before afternoon. Except this yutz!

Raking the hair from his eyes with his fingers, he shoved his feet into his slippers. Then, mumbling invective upon Alexander Graham Bell and his entire progeny, he shambled his way out of the bedroom and over to the desk.

There was another jangle from the phone. It was cut short when he picked it up. "All right. You've got me awake now, so this had better be good. Speak."

What he got was crying and his name said soggily. Recognizing the tears being shed JB wondered, Why me? Why always me?

"Is that you, Len?," he said. There were more tears wrapped around an Uh-huh. "Isn't it too early for you to be this sloshed? Or are you still going from last night?...Len, what are you talking about?.Make some sense!"

After a moment the caller gained some control and JB listened closely to the man's wild ravings. At a pause he jumped in. "All right, Len. Stay where you are. Pour some coffee into yourself and I'll be right there...As soon as I get dressed...Drink coffee ...Lots of coffee."

JB hung up and went to the bathroom for a quick shower. A glance in the mirror proved that all the parts were still there. Two eyes, two ears, a nose, and a mouth. All in a reasonably pleasing arrangement. Not too bad for a forty year old, Upper West Side, New York City, writer-slash-fairy.

While shaving he wondered what kind of mess Len had gotten himself into this time. He was blubbering about blood.

JB slipped his keys onto a back belt loop and put his cash into his front pockets then rushed down the stairs of his apartment building. As he turned toward Columbus Avenue he wondered why he was even going over to Len's. After all, they hadn't been together for almost two years now. But all the things that were attractive about Len were still there. I just can't live with him, JB thought, even if he would stop drinking. And that really had to happen sooner or later.

JB knew from experience that you can't convince a drunk he's a drunk until he's ready to see for himself that he's a drunk. He hailed a cab, got in, and gave the driver an address on the East Side. The ID on the back of the seat gave the driver's name as Aswanary Chandraskhare. He shrugged. So much for conversation on this ride. Instead he thought back....

JB and Len had met at a party. It was one of those usual New York Gay/Yuppie gatherings, with everyone jockeying for position through their jobs, or their wealth, or their infamy.

JB had been invited because his job as a staff writer on a network television game show gave him the degree of status deemed necessary to be accepted by these people. That JB didn't give a pigs-ass about any of the pretentious preppies and what they thought of him didn't seem to faze any one of the deeply shallow guests.

Then Len Matthews arrived. Len was the leading man and star of another network's Gothic-style soap opera. He was then thirty-five years old and handsome in the same way the young Laurence Olivier had turned women's, and quiet a few men's, heads back in the Thirties. Len's eyes were dark, but saved from total black by flecks of another color. His jaw was square, with a cleft that took it just this side of adorable. And there was a head full of wavy auburn hair that in the right light seemed to be afire, with that inevitable, unruly lock tumbling onto his forehead. All of it put together made him perfectly cast as the brooding Lord of Hawthorn Manor, the setting of his soap.

JB was smitten, or struck with lust, one or the other, at once. It took him only minutes to threaten the host into introducing him. JB took it from there.

As his opening salvo JB said, "So, tell me, what's it like waking up every morning knowing you're the fairest in the land?"

The gold flecks in Len's eyes sparkled. Then the corners crinkled and he smiled. JB's heart literally skipped a beat. Len then focused on him with a smidge more interest than before. That little reaction was all JB needed. Finding out about each other was now not only interesting but imperative.

JB could feel the waves of hatred aimed at him from every corner of the party. Especially when, after monopolizing Len for the entire evening, they left together around midnight.

As Len walked JB toward home they talked. They delved into each other's thoughts and feelings, and, lo and behold, found things in common. They passed the awkward stage and went to intimacy before three blocks had passed. Len felt that initial interest turning to attraction.

There was a diner still open at 75th and Broadway. They went in for coffee and stayed until very early. Then Len, after walking JB to his door, hugged him, made a date for that evening, and left. That he hadn't tried to bed JB immediately counted as several points in his favor.

They dated steadily for several months, going to bed the first time after their fifth date. By that time the anticipation had built to such a degree that JB felt like he could impersonate the Michelin Man. It was lucky that Len had the right pin to make him burst.

Len and JB, to all intents and purposes, became lovers, although they didn't live together right away. Len moved into JB's place a year and a half later when his soap was canceled due to falling ratings. Soon after that the troubled times began. Len, at first, had problems getting parts because he was typecast in everyone's mind's as a Gothic hero.

That he wasn't a hero, or even a Goth, led him into a depression. He started to drink. That made him harder to cast. JB tried to ignore Len's increased drinking, but finally couldn't. They argued. A lot. They fought. A lot. After another year of it they decided to live apart.

JB continued to write. The dread of having to return to his hometown and a bit of money saved from his own now canceled game show allowed him to work at his writing full time.

He began working on a short story that ended up becoming a short novel. A murder mystery, of all things. Then he had to market it to someone. The television show on his resume helped and got him read by an editor at a small New York publishing house. He liked it. So the little story that became a little murder mystery became actually published, and thanks to a couple of good reviews and some aggressive publicizing JB won a Silver Magnifying Glass Award as best first novel of that year.

The second mystery sold even better, and JB found himself with an unexpected career that he embraced happily. Len and JB kept in touch. The phone calls when Len was depressed, or morose, or lonely, or happy—but always drunk, angered JB and made Len's problem resoundingly clear.

There were, however, enough remnants of the old Len to keep them close. Len seldom remembered the calls the next day anyway.

JB couldn't think of a time when Len had

sounded so out of control as he had that morning.

No, it was something more. Len was frightened. Which explained why JB was on his way there. With Len talking about blood, JB had to know if he was hurt. If he wasn't then he could calm him down. Either way it was what JB would expect from any of his friends. And, for all the pain in the tush Len was now, or ever could be, he was still his friend.

Once JB noticed the cab had pulled onto Lexington Avenue, not far from Len's place, he told the driver to pull over. He got out, paid, and began to walk the rest of the way.

He relished the crisp cool air that Fall offered the city after a hot and muggy Summer. The sun hung serenely in a clear softly blue sky. The trees, not quiet bare yet, moved gently from a slight breeze. The store windows, behind their webbed safety gates, caught the sun and reflected it back onto the pavement in mosaic like patterns.

Humming a tuneless song, JB turned onto East 64th toward Third. When he was at Len's four-story brownstone, he buzzed the apartment. The door clicked open immediately.

As he went up the stairs, JB spotted Len on the second floor landing. He stood there, unshaven and red-eyed, with a sheet wrapped around his shoulders, American Indian style, motioning JB with a waving of his hand into his room.

Catching the slipping sheet in his other hand he shut the door, leaned against it, and using a gesture last used by Sarah Bernhardt in the year 1887, intoned, "My God, at last you're here. This has been possibly the worst morning of my ill-used life."

JB went over to the windows and threw back the drapes, flooding the studio apartment with light. "It's a beautiful day outside. Why not let it in?"

JB looked around the dishelved studio apartment. It was decorated with mounds of dirty clothes on the floor and accented by stacks of newspapers on practically all the other surfaces. On top of those were unwashed plates, food-caked silverware, and half-filled glasses. A patina of undisturbed dust covered the few bare spots visible among the rubble.

"Don't you ever clean?" JB asked. "I could draw pictures in the dust in here."

Len sat at the table of the utility kitchen on the far wall and covered his eyes against the sunlight streaming into the room. He moaned, "You unmitigated bastard! I've always had a suspicion you were into S&M, but I had no idea you could be this sadistic! My God, that light is so bright! Isn't there a dimmer switch?"

JB shook his head. There was something incomprehensible about a man who can make jokes in the face of a life that is a total disaster. He went to the kitchen cabinet behind Len and looked for a clean cup, ended up washing a dirty one from the pile in the sink, and made coffee from the jar of instant on the counter.

He sat at the table across from the sheet wrapped Len. "Now, what's all the panic about?" he said. "Other than looking like you spent the last week at a camel-herders convention, you don't seem too bad. All your parts look like their still attached. What's this about blood?"

Len looked up, anxiety etched his face. "The bathroom, JB. It's everywhere. On the floor, the walls. It's awful!"

"You're not cut anywhere?"

"No, I'm fine. Just hungover."

JB went to the bathroom, "What caused it then?"

Len didn't move. He wrapped the sheet closer around his body and shouted, "I don't know. I saw the blood. I freaked. So I shut the door and called you."

From inside the bathroom JB exclaimed, "Good Lord!" Then silence. A moment later there was the sound of the shower curtain being pulled aside. "Len! Just what in hell did you do last night?"

Len shook his head. "That's just it. I don't know. I was at the Main Man for Happy Hour, and I think I went down to the Village after. But I can't be sure. I can't remember. What is it, JB?"

JB stood in the doorway, his face pale. "Len, there's a body in there. A dead body."

"What! A body! Oh, God! Did I bring a trick home? I can't remember."

JB went back into the bathroom. A second later he yelled out to Len. "It looks like a suicide. At least the wrists are cut."

"A suicide! Why would a trick kill himself in my bathroom?"

JB came out of the bathroom. "That's no trick," he said. "Unless you've decided to go straight without telling me. The body is a woman."

"What?!"

"Yeah, she's about sixty I'd say. Has on more make-up than any self-respecting drag queen should wear. And her hair. A color no hairdresser ever thought of. Or does Dutch Boy Paints now have a salon formula? And, she's in a fluorescent-pink shorty nightgown. There's even a pair of marabou-trimmed, very high high heels in there. Good taste wasn't the lady's strong point, whoever she might have been."

JB walked back to the kitchen area and leaned against the counter. He looked over at Len. The poor guy looked pitiful. Len's face was colorless. Except for his lips. They were a pale blueish color. His hands were twitching and he couldn't seem to make them stop. Total panic hovered in the corners of his eyes. A barely held in scream rippled his bottom lip.

JB could understand. The blood in the bathroom was spread out like a vampire's picnic. And, that, with a hangover thrown in for good measure, wouldn't make anyone feel like singing *Oh, What A Beautiful Morning.*

JB moved over to Len and gently took his face in his hands. That forced Len to turn his head away from the bathroom doorway. JB looked straight into Len's stricken eyes, "I know you're scared, baby. But you've got to snap out of it. You've got to try to remember what happened last night." He released Len's face. "And we've got to find out who that woman is. So get off your lovely round buns, go in there, and see if you know who she is,"

Len stood, went hesitantly into the bathroom, and came immediately back out. "That's Miss Snoop. She lives upstairs in 3-B." He shook his head. "That's not her real name. I think her name was Sylvia something? Lawton? Luton? No, Lucan. Sylvia Lucan. I called her Miss Snoop because she always had her nose in everyone's business. You know, asking personal questions, listening to other people's conversations. That sort of thing."

JB stopped him. "If she lived upstairs, why would she come here to slit her wrists? And why would you let her in, especially dressed like she is?"

"JB, I'm a man who drinks. When I blackout, as I obviously did last night, Sasquatch could walk in here and rape my refrigerator and I wouldn't know or care about it. What I want to know is what are we going to do now?"

"You know what we have to do. We have to call the police."

Len exploded. "The cops! No. No way! It'll be ugly. They'll think I did it. Can't we keep the police out of this?"

"And what do you plan on doing with her?" JB pointed toward the bathroom. "You can't keep her here like some toy to float in the tub." He paused. "It'll be all right, Len. I have a friend in the department. I'll call him and explain everything." JB went to the phone and started to dial. "Maybe he can help keep it quiet."

"Do you think so?" Len thought for a moment, then asked, "Who's this person you know? And how do you know him?"

"I'm a mystery writer, Len. I meet all kinds of weird people." JB listened to the ringing. "He's a detective. He's helped me with research." The call was connected and a tinny voice said, "Homicide."

"Yes, may I speak with Lieutenant Kelly?" JB waited. The line was answered a moment later. "Hello," a voice growled.

JB said, "Kelly? This is Jeremy Bent. I need your help. And it needs some discretion."

JB hung up. "Kelly will be right here. He said he'd do what he could to keep it quiet. He also said you should stay calm and wait here. I told him that serenity wasn't something you were very familiar with, but since you couldn't take a shower I didn't think you would be going anywhere. You probably should get dressed though. Oh, where is the Super? Kelly thinks I should warn him about the police coming to his building."

"He lives downstairs. In the rear apartment."

"OK. Wash up in the sink there and get dressed. I'll be right back."

JB went down to the rear apartment and knocked on the door. He heard the sound of footsteps coming closer, then the door opened.

JB stood there, his jaw on his chest, stunned. Montgomery Clift was standing in the doorway. Since the actor died in 1966, JB knew it was impossible. But there he was.

The Super was the spitting image of Monty at twenty-five. The same dark hair, sensitive mouth, and deep emotion filled eyes. He was dressed in a T-shirt and a pair of sweat pants that clung tightly to his body, accenting the muscles underneath. JB wanted to ravish him then and there.

That not being a good idea, considering the circumstances, he instead introduced himself, and found out that Monty's real name was Toby Gallo. JB told him about the police coming and asked if he wanted to wait for them upstairs in Len's place.

He nodded, went back inside, and came back in a minute pulling on a sweatshirt that read on the back: *Actors don't really die. It's just a sense memory exercise.*

After locking his apartment Toby started up the stairs. JB followed and filled him in on what happened to Mrs. Lucan the night before.

He also checked out Toby some more. He was quite nicely built. Broad shoulders. Strong legs, and well-defined pecs...along with a pair of the nicest buns JB had seen in quite a while. A fine specimen of a boy. Almost too pretty to be real. But in New York you expected to see the prettiest of them all. They flocked to the city like gaggles of swans.

When they got into Len's apartment Toby went straight for the bathroom. He came back out a few seconds later.

JB asked, "Are you all right?" Toby didn't look very well.

"I will be in a minute." That's Mrs. Lucan for sure. She looks really awful."

"Well, of course, she does. She's dead," Len said.

JB asked Toby, "Can I get you something? A glass of water maybe?"

"Thanks. That might help. I've never seen a dead body before. Are they always so pale?"

Len pursed his lips. "It's because the blood all runs to the lowest part of the body. I'll bet she has the bluest butt on the Upper East Side," he said

"Stop being such a smart ass, Len." JB handed over the water to Toby.

"Well, what did he expect? Angels and Lil' Eva floating up to heaven?"

Toby looked over at JB. "I don't know what I expected. But it wasn't that. How did it happen?"

"A good question," JB answered. "We're not up to how yet. We haven't got past what and who."

"But you can be sure your Lieutenant Kelly will ask how," Len added.

JB had little choice but to agree with Len. A short discussion of the possible outcome of Kelly's questions led the three men to a perplexed silence. They sat and stared at each other and waited for the police to arrive.

Lieutenant Kelly was as good as his word. He arrived twenty minutes after JB's call in an unmarked car. His team parked at the end of the block, and came up the building's back stairway. The men from the coroner's office grumbled, but took the body down the same backstairs on Kelly's orders.

Not many people didn't do what Lieutenant Colin Fitzgerald Kelly told them to do. There was something about him. You just knew you shouldn't upset him. For one thing, no matter what you did to him... dress him up, or down, or put him in a tutu...he still looked like a cop. It was internal. His pores oozed legal process.

Kelly was one of those people who had gone straight from puberty to middle age. His short cut hair was gray. So were his eyes. They looked out on a world he had given up trying to understand years before. He seldom smiled, the mouth was set and rigid. His head sat on his shoulders the same way. He'd always been a cop. From eraser monitor to traffic patrol. From MP to NYPD. He had his reasons for seeming so grim. There was no wonder or magic left for him. Except in one area.

What no one suspected was this cold marble slab of a man had a hunger for art. JB had found this out while he tagged along on a stakeout one night last spring. Two people sitting in a parked car had to talk about something.

Kelly possessed a knowledge and appreciation for art that JB found remarkable. They spent the night talking about painters and their work.

Now, in a rumpled off-the-rack sport coat, he stood in the center of Len's small apartment. His body filled the space, making the room seem uncomfortably crowded.

He watched the three men sitting around him. One of them was nervous, one was curious, and one was a little of both, with a touch of contriteness thrown in for good measure. The Lieutenant could use any one of those attitudes to his advantage. He didn't like bodies showing up where they shouldn't. It disturbed his sense of order. With a little luck he could tie up this case pronto.

He spoke to Toby first. "All right, Mr. Gallo, the coroner's man put the woman's death at approximately two AM. Was there any disturbance around that time? A fight, maybe? Or loud arguing?"

JB looked up, surprised. Toby answered, "No. But, I was asleep by then. I got home late last night. Around midnight. I went out with friends after my show. I'm an actor. At the Dorothy Arzner Playhouse.

I went right to bed when I got in."

Well, I get no luck on this case, Kelly thought. He turned to speak to Len. JB, however, couldn't control his curiosity. "If the lady killed herself, Kelly, why would there have been a disturbance? Slitting your wrists is usually a pretty quiet way to go," he said.

Kelly glared down at JB. "There was a bruise on the victim's jaw, and a bump on the back of her head," he said. "There had to be an altercation of some sort for her to have those." Kelly turned again to Len. "Mr. Matthews, how well did you know the victim?"

"Not very. I spoke to her in the hallway is all. She would collar me and everybody else who lived here." Toby nodded his agreement. "She was always asking about your private business. A regular busybody. I just figured she was lonely."

Toby volunteered, "She was divorced. From some big shot in the art world. She lived alone though."

JB looked up. "I wondered why her name was familiar," he said. "It must be the Lucan Galleries on Madison. That is big."

Kelly nodded and made a note on his pad. He turned back to Len. "Well, why was she in your apartment, Mr. Matthews?" Kelly was like a bulldog. He got a scent and stuck with it.

"If I knew, Lieutenant, I would probably be on a plane to Brazil right now."

"Why is that?"

"Because, if I knew why she was here, it would mean I had something to do with her slitting her wrists. And that would make me an accessory, or something, right?"

"Are you an accessory, Mr. Matthews?"

JB spoke up. "Wait a minute, Kelly. He may be a falling down drunk." Len winced. "And he may have a smart mouth, but he certainly wouldn't beat up on an old woman. He's way too much of a wimp for that."

"Thank you for that glowing personality critique," Len pouted.

Kelly put on his hat. "OK, Bent. But something wonky happened here last night, and I have to find out what. Mr. Gallo, I'll need a list of all the tenants in the building. Mr. Matthews, stay available."

Kelly turned and walked out the door. Toby got up, shrugged, and followed him, shutting the door as he left.

JB turned back to Len. "Sorry about that wimp remark," he said.

"That's all right. Wimp isn't the worst thing you've ever called me. Remember? I think 'vitriolic spawn of Satan's loins' was right up there. You know, a good vocabulary in the wrong hands can make for a prize bitch."

"All right, Len. Point taken."

"JB, what am I going to do? Your Lieutenant thinks I had something to do with that woman's death. I didn't, JB, I...."

"I know you didn't, Len. It is strange though. I just can't figure why she was here in your apartment." He sat at the kitchen table and began to work through the questions in his mind.

"Then you're going to help me?" JB looked up and nodded.

"Great." For several moments Len stood watching his friend thinking. He could almost see the sparks from the gears whirring inside JB's head. "It's so cute when you play Mrs. Polifax," he cracked. He went to the kitchen cabinet, opened the door, and pulled out a bottle of vodka. He poured two fingers into a glass, and drank.

JB went to a stack of newspapers on the desk. He pulled out a copy of *Backstage*, and flipped the pages.

Len asked, "What are you looking for? Better yet, what have you figured out?"

JB didn't look up. "There wasn't any disturbance. Toby didn't hear anything. Your apartment may be messy, but it's lived in mess, not fight mess. That means someone *put* Sylvia Lucan in the bathtub. She didn't crawl in there by herself. Now, even in a blackout, you wouldn't let someone you didn't know into the apartment. That means it had to be someone living in the building. Someone you knew, at least by sight. So, who better would know the peccadilloes of the tenants than the building's Super? What theater did Toby say his play was at?"

Len was about to say something snide about JB being interested more in Toby's peccadilloes than the tenant's when he was cut off.

"Here it is," JB said. "Toby Gallo in a little number called *MINKS RUN*—An exploration into the tortured soul of a commercial mink breeder."

Len looked over JB's shoulder. "Sounds charming. A musical comedy?" He went back to his drink. "The audience is probably more tortured then the minks."

JB laughed. "And you say I'm a bitch. Anyway, any evening spent at the theater can't be all that bad."

"Wantta' bet?" Len said.

"And I can speak with Toby after the play. Do you want to come?"

"No. I think I'll stay here, clean the bathroom, take a shower, and then get pleasantly drunk."

"That's not going to help very much, you know."

"You're probably right, but I'm a falling down drunk, or so you say I am, so I drink. As someone wise once said on a T-shirt. *Reality is an illusion caused by an alcohol deficiency.* There's been way too much reality around here today."

JB was going to add something, but was stopped by Len. "Don't start, JB. We've been down this road before."

"I was only going to say that if it got your apartment cleaned, I guess it's OK."

Len laughed. "You are such a yenta!"

"I think I'm going to get some food into me, and then get ready for the theater. Curtain's at six." JB got his jacket and left the apartment.

Len didn't clean the bathroom, or the apartment, or take a shower. He did get very drunk.

The Dorothy Arzner Playhouse was a second floor sewing machine factory, converted to a loft, changed to a theater, in an industrial building on the upper edge of the Village. It would sit about sixty people on a good night.

It wasn't a good night. There were just ten people, seated in little islands, on metal folding chairs. The chairs stood in four rows back from the foot high platform that served as the stage. JB sat alone in the last row.

Good or bad, JB loved the theater. The atmosphere of even this Off-Off Broadway house filled him with childlike anticipation. It was the Circus, the Zoo, and the State Fair all rolled into one. After a particularly impressive performance he would sit stunned and mute. Sometimes, after a very bad one, he had the same reaction.

Len was right. The play was torture. Most showcases have acting that runs from mediocre too brilliant, and all the levels in between. This one didn't have levels so much as depths.

But Toby stood out. Audience members checked their programs a few minutes into his first scene, just to find out who he was. It could be he actually did have talent, but the play was so badly written and directed it was hard to tell.

JB stopped paying attention around the beginning of Act II. Later, scattered applause woke him from his stupor, and told him it was, at last, over. He left and waited outside.

About thirty minutes later Toby came down the stairs with another of the actors from the play. He noticed JB, said goodnight to his companion, and walked over to where JB stood.

"Mr. Bent? What a surprise! Don't tell me you actually sat through that horror we just performed? You must be a glutton for punishment."

"Please, call me JB. You were very good, considering what you had to work with."

"Thank you," Toby said. He was both pleased and embarrassed by the compliment. There was an extended silence.

To fill that void JB said, "I did have an ulterior motive for coming here tonight. I was kind of hoping you'd have dinner with me?"

A look crossed Toby's face. JB knew it. It had to do with lack of funds. He had been there himself. Before the TV job saved him he had scrabbled from one check to another with no way of being able to partake of any of the chocolate-covered, hand-dipped amusements New York City offered. There was a time when a simple dinner out could blow his budget for weeks.

"It's my treat," JB said. "But if you have other plans?"

"No. I have nothing. That would be great."

"Fine. I know a restaurant just a little way from here. We could walk. It's a nice evening."

Toby nodded enthusiastically.

They walked toward the Village. JB said, "Now, tell me, who directed that play? It was a bank manager, wasn't it?"

Twenty minutes later they stood in front of GAR-BOS. *The restaurant for people who want to be alone* it said on the placard beside the door. They went in, and were seated in a booth along the side of the room.

The décor was subdued, pale pinks and paler blues predominating. Enormous blowups of Greta Garbo, in her various roles, lined the walls. The "Queen Christina" fireplace in the corner emitted a soft glow. Small lamps with fringed shades stood on each table. In a low glass bowl was a camellia in blue tinted water.

The waiter asked for their drink orders. Toby had a beer, JB scotch. The waiter handed them menus, and left them as the placard outside advertised.

"I picked this place so we could talk. I hope that's all right. The food is really excellent."

"Sure. It's fine. What did you want to talk about?" Toby said.

"Well, you for one thing. And that ugly mess from this morning for another."

Toby looked up from his menu. "I didn't have anything to do with that. I told the Lieut...."

"I didn't say you did. What I meant to say was I

wanted to get some information from you, Toby."

"Oh. What sort of information?"

"About the tenants in your building. You see, Len is a very good friend of mine, and I didn't like what Lieutenant Kelly was insinuating this morning. I know Len had nothing to do with Mrs. Lucan's death. But there are some questions that need answering."

"What do you want to know?"

"Tell me about the tenants and what you know about them." JB sat back and watched while Toby gathered his thoughts.

Then Toby said, "So you think it was someone in the building?" JB nodded. "I'll be damned...." Toby leaned against the booth's back and continued. "Well, there's Len, your friend. He's in 2-B. He seems nice enough. Uh....he drinks too much, but he's mostly quiet about it. Keeps to himself. He was an actor, wasn't he? On some soap. Five or six years ago. He was pretty good."

"He was. And could be again if he'd stop the booze."

"Then there was Mrs. Lucan," Toby went on. "She was divorced, like I said this morning. She lived in 3-B. Seemed pretty well off. Alimony, I guess. Lots of nice stuff in her place. Len was right though. She was a busybody. I couldn't prove it, but I think she even went through the building's garbage."

"Humm, that's going a bit beyond just snoopy. Who else?" JB said.

"Well, there's Jenny in 3-A. Jennifer Spring. She claims she's an actress and a model. She could be, she's got the looks. But I've never seen her at any auditions. And she doesn't read the trades. There is this guy that visits. I think he's the boy-friend, and she's the mistress. Now how *Back Street* is that? Above her, in 4-A, there's Mrs. Hamilton Forsyth-Peal. Very social, very upper-crusty, don't you know. I'm sure she disapproves of Jen. I know she disapproves of just about everything else. In 4-B there's a new tenant. Mr. Jones. He just moved in, so I don't know anything about him yet. The apartment was rented by an agent. Him I remember. A big bruiser with short blond hair and a broken nose. He looked like he'd be more comfortable strong arming someone with brass knuckles than doing real estate."

Toby stopped. The waiter had returned with their drinks. While he set them down they gave him their dinner orders. The *Mata Hari* Curry for Toby, The Swedish "Greta" Meatballs for JB. The waiter left them alone once more, and JB turned again to Toby.

"Go on."

"Let's see now, that's the third and fourth floors, and your friend in 2-B. Across from him, in 2-A, there's Professor VonWettering. An old guy. And I mean old. He looks like he could have helped Moses part the waters. I guess he isn't really that ancient, but he must be somewhere in his late seventies. He used to teach at some college here. There are all sorts of framed degrees on his walls. He's retired and pretty unhappy about it. He can be a real pain in my ass that's for sure. Real demanding. Then on the bottom floor, in 1-A, there's this guy, Mr. Terillo, but he's better known on the gay scene as Johnny Huge. You know? The porn star? He thinks no one knows who he is, but I recognized him right off. He's got the garden apartment, so he sunbathes all the time. In the nude. Let me tell you he lives up to his name." Toby gestured Mr. Terillo's penis size by moving his two hands up and down about ten inches apart. JB raised his eyebrows.

Toby nodded with an appropriate leer, then went on. "I'm sure that makes me sound like a peeping Tom, but how can you not check something like that out, right? Anyway, in the other apartment, 1-B, there's these two guys. They're not gay, at least I don't think they are. But they share the rent. They are what I'd call fashion victims, if they weren't already beyond that. Whatever's in, they have one of, maybe two. Trend-sucking little nits. God knows what they do to make a living. They're always home during the day." Toby paused a moment, then went on. "And I live in the rear apartment, by myself, and you know about me." He blinked and smiled.

I don't know nearly enough, JB thought. I have a whole lot more to learn about you, cupcake. But let's not be too obvious about it, OK, JB? He asked, "So, were any of the tenants more friendly than any of the others with Mrs. Lucan?" That'll throw Toby off the track for a little while.

Toby shook his head. "Not really. All of us just kinda put up with her. She flirted with the Professor sometimes. But he wasn't interested. It really was sorta funny. She'd get all fancied up and knock on his door with cookies or something. He would take them, then practically slam the door in her face. The other tenants just looked pained when she was around."

"It must have been hard for her, to be that disliked."

"If she even knew she was. She didn't act like it. She was always chirping around, happy as a lark, pecking at everything and everybody." Toby stopped. "That's really about all I know. Sorry it isn't more."

"No," JB said, staring again at the thick lashes that surrounded Toby's dark brown eyes. "You've been a great help. Now, why don't you tell more about yourself? Have you always wanted to be an actor?"

Toby looked down at his hands. Then he looked up and smiled across the table. JB smiled back.

It was that damn phone again; JB sat up in bed and checked the bedside clock. "Seven A.M.! This is getting ridiculous." He hurried to answer it because he didn't want to disturb Toby's sleep. Toby was lying, warm and cozy, in the spot JB had just left.

JB picked up the phone and before he could say a word Len started to speak. JB listened for only a moment. "You know, Len, this is the second time in as many days you've woke me up early. If this keeps up you're going to make me cranky. And if I get cranky you're going to lose some body parts you might find very precious!"

JB could hear sounds coming from the bedroom. Then Toby stood, nude, in the doorway, rubbing sleep from his eyes. They smiled at each other.

"What did you say, Len?" His attention was drawn back to the conversation. "I'm sorry, I wasn't listening.... What?....How can they think that?....All right, I'll come down....Just wait....And, Len, don't say anything that could get you in more trouble."

When JB hung up Toby asked, "What's he need a lawyer for?"

"The police have him at the station. For questioning about the murder of Mrs. Sylvia Lucan."

"I thought she slit her wrists."

"So did I, but apparently the preliminary autopsy showed the wounds were inflicted by someone else."

"Wow. And they think Len did it?"

"Well, they've got him at the station, so he must be a suspect. But that's crazy. Len wouldn't hurt anybody. Except himself. I have to go down there."

Toby moved from the doorway to where JB stood. He wrapped both his arms around him and kissed him on the cheek, then on the mouth. He said, "Can't you go about twenty or thirty minutes from now?"

JB felt himself getting hard. "I don't suppose it will hurt Len to stew a while longer. Maybe he'll learn to stop calling so damn early."

They smiled and returned to the bedroom.

Lieutenant Kelly wasn't happy. His leading suspect in this suicide that had turned out to be a murder not only couldn't remember where he was the night it happened, but couldn't even come with a reason for the body being in his apartment. And, to make it worse, his mystery writer friend had come to his aid like Renfield of the Mounties.

Right now Bent was pacing back and forth across his office while Matthews sat looking dejected at his desk.

Kelly broke the silence. "Let me get this straight. You say you have no alibi?"

JB answered for Len. "He said he doesn't remember. That's different. He also said he thought he went down to the Village. Why don't you check out the bars there? One of the bartenders might remember him."

"We plan too, Bent," Kelly said, then turned back to Len. "I have to say this doesn't look good for you, Matthews. Right now you're our only suspect."

JB had enough. Kelly was trying to scare Len into saying something, anything, that could incriminate him. He said, "Then again, it can't look all that bad either, since there is no earthly reason for him to have murdered the woman. How about her ex-husband? I understand she lived pretty well. Maybe he wanted to get out of paying her alimony?"

"A possibility. Bent. We'll look into it. Matthews, it might be a good idea to call your lawyer."

Len looked up. "I already called. He should be here soon. I want out of here, JB."

"I know you do, Len. The lawyer will help."

Kelly said, "All right. If your lawyer's on his way I'll hold off asking anymore questions until he gets here. I can't do more than that, Bent."

"Thanks, Kelly." JB put his hand on Len's shoulder. "You'll be out of here soon. When you're released, why don't you go on home? I'll talk to you later."

Len mouthed a thank you to JB as he prepared to go. Then Len looked over at Lieutenant Kelly. "Will I be able to get out of here?"

"Since we can't hold you on suspicion, you probably will. Oh, Bent, the victim's ex? It was Helmut

Lucan, right? You mentioned him yesterday."

JB stopped at the door. There wasn't much that got by Kelly. "So you did hear me. That's right. Hulmut Lucan. He's a big shot in the art world. You must know his gallery over on Madison?"

Kelly did know it. He'd even been in it a few times.

The gallery showed mostly Impressionists and mid-nineteenth century artists. Not always the best quality works, considering the outrageous prices, but good enough to earn Lucan a mostly solid reputation. There was some talk, a few years back, about fake Mattisse's and bogus Monet's being shown as real. There wasn't any real proof, but the rumors still hung on.

"Yeah, I know it. And I know about him. He's a razor sharp businessman and a vicious opponent when he's after a painting he wants. He drove another dealer into bankruptcy just to get a Degas he coveted."

"Well, even Mary Poppins could be a bitch when she didn't get her way. You know, it's just possible Mrs. Lucan was even sharper than Mr. Lucan, and he couldn't stand it."

"I'll check it out," Kelly said, the irritation clear in his voice. "But first, there's paperwork to be done and reports to get back from the coroner and the lab. Then we have to correlate the data and assign the team their tasks. After that...."

"None of which helps Len a whole hell of a lot," JB said. He turned the doorknob and left the office.

JB stood in front of a heavy smoked glass door. Down on the lower right hand corner, in gold-leaf block letters, were the words: LUCAN GALLERIES. Under that, in script, was the name: *Helmut Lucan.* Under that, again in block letters, was the word:

Proprietor. This was the only indication on the storefront of what lay inside. It was understated to such a degree as to be pretentious and pushy even on Madison Avenue, one of America's pushier avenues.

When JB stepped inside he found the galley self-consciencely elegant and sophisticated. It had thick plum colored carpet, light gray walls, and chrome accents. The precise lighting screamed out in a language all its own. It was the language of money, and it asked *If you don't have any, why are you here?*

He stood for a few minutes and was finally approached by an officious young man who spoke with what could not be a real British accent. JB told him his name and asked to see the owner. The young man looked him up and down, sniffed, and indicated he would tell the exalted Mr. Lucan of his presence.

JB curled his upper lip at the phony little snobette's back then looked around at the paintings hung ever so carefully on the walls. There were a few pieces by the great artists, Gauguin and Manet among them, and many lesser artists of the period were also represented. Each was lit with great care as they quietly told of an age long ago. An age more concerned with gentle beauty than our own current frantic environment. In a far corner he found a small Toulouse-Lautrec sketch to admire.

"You have excellent taste, Mr. Bent." The voice, coming from behind him, was distinctly cultured and modulated to a soft treble.

JB turned and saw a tall, well-dressed man somewhere in his mid-sixties. His silver hair was cut and groomed to within an inch of its life. His skin testified to hours spent under lights at the tanning salon. His dark pinstripe suit was expensive and impeccably tailored. He smiled what was supposed to be an ingratiating smile and said, "I'm Helmut Lucan. How may I help you? Does the sketch interest you?"

"It's a wonderful piece," JB answered. "But out

of my range, I'm afraid."

"I'm sure some kind of arrangement could be worked out for the sketch."

"Don't tempt me, Mr. Lucan. Please. Actually, there is another reason for my wanting to meet with you."

"And what is that?"

"Uh...this is difficult, Mr. Lucan. It seems your wife died last Sunday morning. The police are calling it murder. A friend of mine is being blamed. I'm sorry to bring such bad news."

Lucan didn't turn a lacquered hair, but his eyes narrowed down to thin slits. "There is no reason to be sorry, Mr. Bent. My ex-wife and I had little to nothing to do with each other."

"Then you and she didn't get along?"

"What we did, Mr. Bent, was quite simply, loathe each other. You see, Sylvia has—I should say had I suppose. Anyway, she had an amazing ability to make her life miserable. And an equal ability to make anyone who came in contact with her just as miserable. Especially me."

Lucan's heretofore placid façade began to crack as he warmed to his subject. His voice took on a hard edge. "She was a vile, contemptible, and vulgar woman, Mr. Bent. Perhaps the happiest day of my life was the day our divorce was final. It meant she was out of my life forever."

"Not completely. What with alimony and all."

Lucan laughed. He meant it to sound wicked but it came out sounding like a mean-spirited giggle. "That was one of the few good things about the whole affair. I had made her sign a pre-nuptial agreement. Other than a far too generous settlement she got nothing."

"Really," JB said. "When was the last time you saw her?"

By now Lucan had only the last few tattered remnants of his previously elegant demeanor. "Just once after she was gone. There were some articles missing from my home. Important articles, I might add. I wanted them back. I confronted her and the evil slut laughed at me. The bitch taunted me with *Finders-keepers, Losers-weepers.* I wanted to thrash her, but even when I am that angry I won't hit a woman. Not even that ugly, spiteful, dreadful, woman."

"Why didn't you go to the police? If the articles were valuable they could have recovered them for you."

JB's mention of the police seemed to make Lucan put out a concentrated effort to calm himself. He forced his hands to unclench. He strained to smooth out his breathing. "The articles only had small personal value, Mr. Bent." His voice was still a bit shaky. "I apologize for my lack of control. I'm afraid Sylvia always brought out the worst in me. It was amazing how she could do that. She once pissed off a Buddhist monk."

JB decided that getting out of the gallery was better than asking any more questions. Why upset this guy more? There was an anger hovering around him, like a rain cloud about to drench everyone in the vicinity. It didn't seem a good idea to continue to set off this particular monsoon. "And thank you for your time." A quick handshake and JB was out of there.

Lucan watched him leave. There was a look of profound worry on his face.

The buzzer let JB through the lobby door and into the building. Toby stood, smiling, at his door at the end of the hall. As he walked toward him, JB was struck again by how handsome he was. And how young.

Someone this age isn't my usual type, JB thought. A man a few years too old for the military draft is more normal. If nothing else, there are mutual memories to fill in those times when talking becomes necessary. The young don't appreciate the past. It makes sense, they have no past to speak of. The young only look forward. It isn't until the familiar is replaced by the new that you value what came before. How do you make the young understand the silky smooth tones of a Patsy Cline? Or, the way *If Your Going To San Francisco, Be Sure To Wear Some Flowers In Your Hair* spoke to a generation? How do you explain Ish Kabbible? The young think Sputnik was a radical movement between Beatniks and Hippies. That Spiro was fourth after Groucho, Harpo, and Chico. They don't believe that he was vice-president of the United States. There just isn't any common ground. No magic words to trigger the past. You say, "Pluck your magic twanger, Froggie" to anyone under thirty and they think you're talking dirty.

JB's thinking stopped when Toby grabbed him and planted a hard kiss on his mouth. The kind of kiss that stirred not memories, but his cock.

Toby pulled JB into his apartment. He whispered, "What a surprise! You should stop by every day." They kissed again.

JB felt Toby's hard body press against his. His fingers traced the line of Toby's jaw, the hollows of his neck, the curve of his spine. I am totally and completely powerless over the male physique, he thought. His hands roamed the roundness of Toby's butt. He felt the hardness of Toby's crotch press against his and realized that his was equally hard.

Toby moved his lips to nuzzle JB's neck. He unbuttoned his shirt and ran his tongue over his skin. He tasted the mixture of soap and natural salt on JB's chest and stomach. JB caught his breath, then said an ecstatic, "Yes."

Toby dropped to his knees.

Fifteen minutes later, Toby looked into JB's slack and contented face "Are you hungry? I can fix lunch?"

JB nodded. He was sure his voice would squeak if he said anything. Toby went to the kitchenette, got bread and deli roast beef, made sandwiches, poured iced tea, and set it in front of JB. Then he took the seat opposite.

What with lingering looks, smiles and laughter, it took them close to an hour to get through the simple meal.

Then they went to bed.

After another half-hour they lay contented in each other's arms. Toby broke JB's glow by asking. "Were you able to help Len this morning?"

"Actually, he should be home soon. You can't hold someone on suspicion."

"How about affection?"

"Then you hold on for dear life," JB said. They kissed. "I do want to ask you a favor."

Toby stretched out his lithe body. "If this afternoon is a sample, you can have my favors anytime you want."

"I might hold you to that, but it isn't what I meant," JB said, ruffling Toby's hair. They heard the lobby door open and someone go quickly up the stairs to the second floor.

"I'll bet that's Len." JB sat up and began to put his clothes on. "I have to talk to him."

When he'd dressed JB looked over at Toby still lying in bed. He leaned over and kissed his cheek. "How would you like to have dinner at my place later? We can watch a movie too."

"Sure. I'd like that."

"Great. You bring the video. Pick out something fun. And I'll supply the pizza. Do you like pepperoni?" Toby nodded his agreement happily. "Now, about that favor I was going to ask."

When Len answered JB's knock, he looked him up and down and arched an eyebrow. "Well, hello," he said. "I expected to hear from you but not in person."

"I had lunch with Toby downstairs. When I heard you come in, I came right up."

"From the look on your face, I'd say food wasn't the main item on the menu. There's nothing like the first few days of an affair to make even the most normal person look like PeeWee Herman on acid. You, however, just look downright silly." Len turned and went to the table where a *Daily News* was spread out.

"It's called happy, Len. If you try real hard you'll remember it." JB looked around the still messy room and shook his head. Then he made a tsking sound.

"I know, Mother. I called a service. They're sending someone over this afternoon to clean."

JB went to the table and sat. "Well, you should plan on a huge tip, because he'll deserve it. What's in the papers? Anything about the murder?"

"That's exactly why I bought it. It's the same old thing though. Inflation is up. Politicians are crooks. Donald Trump just bought something else. That escaped killer, Willie Hackshaw, is still at large. It's been two weeks without a lead. But there's nothing about Mrs. Lucan. Even on the inside pages. Thank God."

"By the way, I stopped at the Lucan Galleries after I left you."

"Well, give. What did he say?"

"His opinion of his ex-wife isn't very high. Utter and complete hatred are the words that come to mind. And, he said she didn't get any alimony. But Toby said she lived pretty well. So, where did she get her money?"

Len said, "Stocks and bonds? Or maybe she had a sugar daddy?"

"Considering the way people seem to have felt about her it would have had to be Atilla the Hun. Anyway, Toby said she was after the old guy across the hall from you. Stocks and bonds? Maybe. We'll find out." JB got up and went to the door.

"What do you mean?"

"I mean we've got to check out her apartment." He opened the door. "Are you coming?"

Len followed him to the hall. JB was on the second step of the staircase. "Isn't this called breaking and entering?"

JB turned. "Toby gave me the key to the apartment. How can you be breaking and entering when you have the key?" He continued up the stairs.

Len hesitated a moment, then followed. On the third floor he found JB at Mrs. Lucan's door inserting the key. "So we're only entering," Len said. "Great. That only makes us half-criminals."

JB reached inside the apartment, flipped the light switch, and stepped inside. Len looked quickly behind him for any witnesses, found none, and followed JB by a step. He was stopped by JB's back. "Move in, damn it!" JB took another step inside and Len shut the door. He turned and his jaw dropped.

JB said, "From the way she was dressed the other morning I expected the place to look like a Chinese bordello. But I didn't expect anything like this." Len nodded dumbly.

The apartment, a living room with a bedroom beyond, was exquisite. The décor was no particular style, but was a mix of eclectic pieces, all of them antiques. Track lights illuminated the Bauhaus and Art Deco furniture. The walls were covered in a pale tan suede. On one wall hung a small-spotlighted painting, displayed as if it was a jewel, with an elegant gilt frame as its setting. In fact, the entire apartment had the feeling of a display window at Bergdorfs department store.

A sculpture, in black granite, sat on a lighted pedestal in the corner. The antique carpets were angled precisely to pull the room into one cohesive unit. On the tables were smaller objet d'art. A Faberge egg here, a Lalique bowl there. On the far wall, between the damask-draped windows, stood a Paul Poiret nineteen-twenties desk. JB walked to the desk and began to open its drawers at random. Len was still standing at the door looking at the apartment. Then, with a hand on each hip, said, "JB, this place is incredible! That furniture is to die for. The Deco style is just beginning to be collectible. And the art! I haven't seen this much outside a museum, ever. That sculpture is a Noguchi!" He moved across the room to the wall. "And this painting. My God, it's a Monet!"

"You've got to be wrong, Len. It can't be. It has to be a print."

He peered at the painting closely. "I don't think so, JB."

JB went to where Len stood in front of the shimmering little painting. "It's got to be. If it were original it would be worth millions."

"Millions or not, this looks like the real thing. Look at the brush strokes." He bent to look at the lower corner. "And the signature. Monet. 1894. I may not be an expert, but I've been to the Modern Museum. This work looks like theirs."

"But where did she get it?"

Len moved around the room inspecting the other objects. "Maybe from her ex? He is a dealer"

"No. He said she only got a settlement. He did say she had stolen some items from him. But they only had small personal value to him. At least that's what he said. I mean, a genuine Monet is sure as hell more than that."

"JB, no matter what you say, all of this is real. The egg, the bowl, all of it. Even the furniture is real antiques. I wonder who her decorator was?"

"Where did she get the money? That's what I want to know." JB returned to the desk. He opened the center drawer. "Ah-ha, bankbooks." He pulled them out. "This might shed some light." A moment later he blew a low whistle.

Len asked, "What? She didn't have a dime, right? All of this is stolen. I'll bet she was a cat burglar on the side. See, you're not the only one who can write mysteries."

"Don't give up your day job. Put together she had about sixty-five thousand in the bank. Twenty thousand in her checking account alone." He rifled the pages. "All put in as large deposits. Ten thousand and twenty thousand at a time. The last one a few days ago. But not regular, at odd times. I can't figure it."

"Please tell me that was a gift," Len said, pointing at a large lidded urn by the sofa. "That looks like something out of one of those Fifth Avenue schlock shops. And it's huge. It's totally out of place in this room."

"Don't critique it, Len. Look in it."

"For what? Ugly dust?" He lifted the lid.

"No. For papers, books, a diary. Anything to explain how she got all this."

"Nope. Nothing in it." He replaced the lid.

"Well, keep looking," JB said.

They searched everywhere. They checked behind the picture. Under the base of the sculpture. Inside the pedestal. They took their time and searched with the eyes of a Tiffany's security guard so they wouldn't miss anything. They checked each piece of furniture.

Inside. Under. Between. They fingered each cushion and throw pillow. They looked through each drawer. Behind and in every book. And still they found nothing.

When they opened the louvered doors to the bedroom, JB looked around. "Now this is more like it."

"My Lord! There should be burning incense and a eunuch in the corner," Len said.

Red flocked wallpaper covered the walls. A round bed sat against the far wall, surrounded by heavily tasseled and swaged draperies. Painted plaster statues of turbaned blackamoors, with lampshades over their heads, stood on each side holding the swags in place. On the floor was a white fake-fur carpet cut in an animal shape. On the ceiling a block of gold-veined mirror tiles reflected the unmade bed. The bed had rumpled black satin sheets and a white taffeta quilted spread. An open magazine was in the center of the monstrosity. JB picked it up.

Len said, "Not a very restful room, is it?"

"I don't think rest is what she planned the room for," JB answered. He handed the magazine to Len.

Len turned the pages and found pose after pose of nude men and women in various and graphic sexual positions. "So, what we have here is an art connoisseur with the soul of a whore."

"What we have here is a horny old lady. Put the book down and let's check out the room."

"JB, I think I'm afraid of what I'll find."

"Just leave any whips, chains, or vibrators where you find them, and you'll be fine."

Twenty minutes later JB stood in the living room; the question mice in his head were running around the maze again. He heard Len come in from the bedroom and looked up expectantly.

Len shook his head. "Nothing. Except for a closet full of the tackiest clothes I've ever seen. Stuff only a hooker could love."

"Well, that doesn't help. What doesn't wash is that kind of taste there." He pointed to the bedroom. "With this kind of taste here."

"You know what all of this is? Other than art, I mean. They're investments. All of this furniture and things are up and coming collectibles. Every one of these items could be sold for a profit. More than what she paid for them anyway. The collector's market has been crazy lately."

"Len, I could kiss you." JB went to the desk, picked up the bankbooks and looked through them again. "Yup, right after each of the deposits, except the last one, there were withdrawals. That's when she bought all this."

"So? Mrs. Lucan was an art dealer just like her ex-husband."

"And that's no reason to get murdered. I take back my kiss."

Len was watching JB lock Mrs. Lucan's front door. Then from behind him a melodious breathy voice said, "Do you always go wandering through dead people's apartments?"

"We're got!" Len theatrically clutched at his heart and leaned against JB. When he had recovered enough to turn to see his accuser, he breathed a sigh of relief. "Oh, it's only you. My God, woman, you do know how to scare a body."

"I'm sorry. I didn't mean to."

Len smiled weakly. "It'll be OK. This body of mine

has had worse shocks done to it. JB, this is Jenny. She lives over there in 3-A."

"Hello. I'm Jeremy Bent. But everyone calls me JB."

"It's really Jennifer. Not Jenny. Jennifer Spring."

She lived up to her name. She had the same fresh, youthful promise of the season itself. She was, by any standard, beautiful. And, even with the artifice of make-up, there was still an engaging innocence about her.

She asked, "So, what were you doing in the old biddy's apartment?" Her voice had the same quality that Marilyn Monroe cultivated for her career. A whisper mixed with one part sweetness and two parts pure sex.

"Trying to find out some answers to a few questions," JB said.

"Like why she killed herself?"

Len said, "You haven't heard? She was really murdered."

Jennifer's already large eyes opened wide. "No kidding? I'm not surprised though. She was a mean old thing."

"Do you mind if I asked you a few questions?"

"Why? I don't know anything."

JB explained, "These things are worked out by gathering little bits of information. Maybe not even related by themselves. But put together they make a complete picture."

Jennifer smiled. "Oh, like a jigsaw puzzle. I do those. They're fun." She leaned her head over to one side and smiled again. With her round sweet face and dimpled chin she looked for all the world as if she was doing an impression of Shirley Temple as a child star. Or even later as an Ambassador. *Heidi of Sunnybrook Farm Goes To Bangladesh.*

"Right," JB said evenly. "And your pieces might help."

She righted her head, put a fingernail to her mouth and chewed for a moment. This concentration on her part caused little folds to appear between her bewildered looking green eyes. Finally she made up what passed for her mind. "Well, all right. If you think I can help I'll try. Come on in." She opened her handbag, and after a search through the depths of it, got out her key. She opened the door of her apartment and bounced inside.

JB put his hand on Len's arm. Len nodded and whispered, "She really is sweet, but a whole lot on the dumb blond side."

"But she's a brunette...."

"With blond roots."

Jennifer popped her head out the door. "Are you two coming in or not?" She went back inside. JB and Len followed.

She sat on the couch. JB sat next to her. Len took a chair opposite.

"Now," she said. "What do you want to know?" She seemed eager to please. If she were a puppy her little tail would have been wagging about sixty miles an hour.

"You didn't like Mrs. Lucan very much, did you?"

The tail wagging stopped. "Noooo, I didn't," she cautiously replied. "How did you know?"

This could be difficult, JB thought. He explained, "You called her a 'biddy' and 'a mean old thing'." She blinked. "Out in the hall. A few minutes ago."

A light went on. She'd come home. "Oh, yeah. Well, yes. She was. Mean, I mean." Jennifer giggled at her play on words. "She was always saying nasty things to me."

"Like what?"

"Oh, that I was stupid. Or that I wouldn't come in out of the rain. That's silly. I always get out of the rain. It ruins your hair." She patted her shoulder length example.

Yes, JB decided, this was going to be very difficult. "I can see where it would. On the night she died, did you hear or see anything?"

"Well, I saw Andy."

"Who's Andy? Does he live in the building?"

"No, silly. Andy's my boyfriend. He was here that night. He doesn't like her either. Mrs. Lucan. She made nasty remarks to him too. About boffing a bimbo. Things like that."

"So you two were here in the apartment all night?" She nodded. "And you didn't hear anything?" Her nail went to her mouth again. She was concentrating. Thinking really shouldn't be that hard, JB decided. A moment later she said, "I did hear one thing."

"What?"

"The radio. The station did a tribute to the Dixie Cups. The fifties girl group? It was neat."

OK, that's it, JB thought, this is too difficult. "I can't think of anything else I need to ask. Can you Len?"

Len shook his head. His eyes had a glazed over look about them. JB said, "Thank you, Jennifer. "You've been a great help."

"Really?" She actually patted her hands together "Oh, I'm so glad."

JB and Len got up and went to the door.

"Can I ask a question?," she said

JB looked back. "Of course."

"What's a boff?"

Outside in the hall JB had a bemused look on his face. "Toto, why do I feel like I just got back from the Land of Oz?"

"Because ya did, Blanche, ya did," Len said

mixing his movie clichés. "I think I need a drink." He headed toward the stairs.

JB hurried behind and caught him on the first step. "No, you don't," JB said. "It's only three PM. Its way too early to start drinking. And there are other apartments to talk to."

"JB, why do you think I want to see these people?" Len found himself being pulled across the landing and up the stairs.

"Len, the way you're carrying on you would think you were living in a circus sideshow. First the Bimbo, and now what? Dumbo?"

They stopped in front of apartment 4-A and JB rang the bell. When the door opened and he saw who answered, he would swear he heard the sound of a calliope floating somewhere in the background.

In the doorway was this enormous striped tent of a dress filled by an equally huge woman. She was so large JB looked down to make sure there wasn't another set of legs standing under her dress hem. One set of elephantine calves tapered down to a pair of tiny thin ankles. They looked as if they would snap if their owner put on one more ounce.

On the lady's head was a cap of little bouncy curls. A poodle-cut gone a faded champagne blond. The style was a refuge for those who were unable to lift fat arms up to their heads with a comb. Somewhere on her face there had to be cheekbones, but they were completely lost in the excess adipose tissue. Pale dun-colored eyes peered out of a suet-pudding face.

From a cupid-bow painted mouth, which seemed way too small to take in the amount of food necessary to cause this degree of obesity, she said, "May I help you?" The voice was high pitched and girlish.

JB said, "Yes, Ma'am. We were wondering if you had time to answer a few questions about Mrs. Lucan?"

She played with a double strand of marble sized pearls that hung between her head and shoulders in the area usually called a neck. She, however, had a column of chins. "You don't mean that vulgar woman from downstairs? The one who killed herself."

Len said, "Yes, Mrs. Peal. But she didn't kill herself. She was apparently murdered."

She dropped the pearls from plump fingers as her face managed to jiggle into an expression of surprise. "Oh, how ghastly. Do come in. I must have details." She stepped back. "And the name is Forsyth-Peal. Mrs. Hamilton Forsyth-Peal the Third, to be exact."

She turned on her substantial heel and waddled into the apartment. JB and Len followed her inside. They watched as she turned and carefully eased herself into a large overstuffed chair. Then they stared as her body reformed and shivered down after her as if the rolls of fat were living separate lives of their own. When all had settled she looked up. "Now, what is it you wish to know?"

She reached over to the table beside her chair and picked out a piece from a box of chocolates kept there. She bit into it, looked at it with distaste, shrugged, and popped it into her mouth. Her chewing made the chins under her jaw slap together rhythmically. JB continued to stare at her fascinated.

Len then took up the slack and said, "We were wondering if you heard anything that morning? Anything at all?"

"Why, no. Nothing. But, it doesn't surprise me one little bit that she was murdered. She was a dreadful woman. An absolute tart. That sort always comes to a bad end. Always."

"Quite right, quite right." In response to the blatant snobbery of Mrs. Forsyth-Peal Len had begun to sound like your stereotypical British Lord something or upper-other. "Would you mind, awfully, telling us your whereabouts on the evening of Mrs. Lucan's demise?"

Mrs. Forsyth-Peal started to warm toward Len. She must have thought she had found a kindred soul. She smiled toothily in his direction. "Let me check my book. Young man, would you be so kind?" She pointed, without looking at JB, toward a Vitton notebook on the table against the wall. He went over, picked it up, and handed it to her.

She flipped through it, searching for the right evening. "Yes, here it is. Saturday. We dined at the Bickfords. They are such a lovely couple. Do you know them?" She aimed another toothy smile in Len's direction. "After the meal, they had a musicale with Madam Clara Chazlaskya. The Mezzo. Quite bewitching. It went quite late. Ham, that's my husband, and I didn't arrive home until after one in the morning. We had a nightcap and went to bed right after. What an exhausting evening it was."

Len smiled broadly. "It sounds positively stygian!"

Mrs. Forsyth-Peal had a confused look for a moment, then decided to fake it. "Oh, it was. It was."

Len looked over at JB. He was trying mightily to stifle his laughter. "Jeremy," Len said sharply. "Is there anything else we need to know from this extremely kind lady?" He smiled at her. JB shook his head. "Fine," Len continued in his British Lord pompous accent. "Then we'll leave you, Mrs. Forsyth-Peal. Thank you for your help in this decidedly distasteful matter."

"That's quite all right. It has been most enjoyable meeting you. Do come again, won't you please."

"That would be lovely," Len answered. "Ta-ta." He walked to the door and waited for JB to open it. When JB did, he turned to give Mrs. Forsyth-Peal a patently false grin, and they exited.

Out in the hall, softly so Mrs. Forsyth-Peal wouldn't hear, Len and JB giggled as though they were a pair of schoolgirls at a church social.

"Ta-ta! You are not a nice person Len Matthews. Putting that poor woman on like that."

"She's such a phony. And she deserved what she got. I detest social climbers."

JB looked across at the other door, "Who's in 4-B?"

"I thought that apartment was empty."

"No, Toby did say someone had moved in a week ago."

"Well, I haven't seen him. Maybe he's invisible."

"Or Claude Raines," JB said as he rang the buzzer next to the door.

It has got to be a joke, JB thought to himself. The door to apartment 4-A opened and he couldn't believe what was standing in the doorway. Somehow Len had set this up. That, or his eyes were completely deceiving him. It was a reaction to what he had said to Len just a few moments ago. That had to be it.

Standing in the doorway was a quiet reasonable facsimile of the aforementioned Claude Raines as *The Invisible Man*. This ghost of a movie studio past wore a dark cotton robe over pajamas. Leather slippers covered his feet. White cotton gloves covered the hands. What was most shocking was the man's head. Covered entirely in bandages, wrapped round and round, you couldn't see either his face or his hair. All you saw was a mound of white that reminded JB of a sinister Q-tip. Over the space where the man's eyes peered out was a pair of dark sunglasses.

If this guy speaks with a British accent, JB thought, I want out of here.

From a slit in the gauze a rough muffled voice said in pure Brooklyn-ese, "What da hell do ya want?"

JB, relief in his own voice, said, "I'm sorry to disturb you, sir. My friend and I..." JB indicated Len, whose eyes were open as wide as his also dropped jaw. "...would like to ask you a few questions. If you don't mind?"

The man's hand went inside his robe at chest level. He growled, "I do mind. Can't ya see I'm convalesin'?"

"I can see. But I won't take up much of your time. I just wanted to know if you knew anything about Mrs. Lucan's death. You know, the woman who was killed yesterday?"

"Killed! I don't know nuthin'. So fuck off!" He stepped back and slammed the door.

JB turned and looked at Len. "I think we just met someone even Will Rogers would not have liked," Len said.

"Well, he certainly doesn't want to get to know anyone. Not very neighborly, is he?"

They went over to the stairs and began to go down.

JB stopped midway. "Did you see what he was wearing under that robe? I could swear there were bulges from leather straps."

"Leather! That's so quaintly perverse. Maybe we should go back. There might be some sort of Red Cross orgy going on in there. I would hate to miss it."

"I don't think so, you hedonist. The straps belong

to a shoulder holster. And there was a bulge under his left arm. He was carrying a gun."

"A gun? Are you sure?"

"I know it doesn't make much sense, but that's what I saw."

They continued down the stairs, passed the third floor, and onto the stairs to the second.

"What do you suppose the bandages were all about?" Len asked.

"With that attitude of his, someone probably threw acid at him."

"And they're still trying to get him. That's why he has a gun."

"Len, you've got to give up this delusion that you can write plots. That's right out of an old-time penny dreadful."

On the second floor landing they saw a man standing in front of Len's apartment door. He was tall and had a Neanderthal-like build. There was a blocky body with to long arms and a square-jawed mostly handsome face. He wore a pair of tight jeans and running shoes. The massive upper torso was covered by a T-shirt and a cardigan style sweater. Put together with the crewcut blond hair he looked like a slightly too old college jock. Like he'd been put back several grades.

Len called out, "Are you the man from the agency?"

The man turned quickly, and with a surprised look on his face nodded yes. "Great. I'll open up for you. The cleaning stuff is under the sink. The vacuum is in the closet by the door. I'll be in the building if you need anything, otherwise I'll leave you to your duties."

By now the jock looked more confused than surprised, but his eyes did check Len out. First the face, then down to check the size of Len's basket, than back to the face. It's the same evaluation look that generations of gay men have perfected to a science. Horny-ology. He smiled. "You don't have to leave on my account. I'd like the company."

Len opened the door to his apartment. "I couldn't stay. I'd be in your way."

The jock walked into the room as Len pulled the door shut on him. He turned to JB. "Am I mistaken, or was I just cruised?"

"You were not only cruised, honey, but done, cum, and hearing *Was it good for you?* after his eyes got finished."

"Humm. He was sorta cute. And I would like a drink."

"Too beefy for my taste. I'm trying to cut down on red meat. Anyway, if you went in there you'd never get the place cleaned. Why don't we talk to another tenant?"

Len heaved a resigned sigh. "All right, if we must. Who's next?"

"Professor Leslie VonWettering, Ph.D.," JB read from the card above the doorbell. "He's a professor, so it can't be that bad. What's he like?"

As JB pushed the button, the bing, bong, bong, bing of a set of chimes rung out. Over them Len said, "If he were an actor he could play the portrait in the last scene of Dorian Gray."

The door opened and JB looked into blank space. He heard someone from somewhere around his waist, say, "Yes?" JB looked down. Standing there was a wizened old man. Like many old people the years had neutered him so that he resembled somebody's grandmother. His tiny eyes peered suspiciously out of a face that was a landscape of lines, furrows, and crevasses, like a riverbed in a drought. He had a full head of thin wavy white hair, yellow on the tips. On his bent over body he wore a crumpled, baggy suit gone out of style twenty years before. His hands were small, bony, and covered with age spots.

"Vhat can I do for you?" His voice was frail and as wrinkled as his face. He had a slight accent mostly affecting his W's.

Len stepped forward. "We were wondering if we could speak to you, Professor. My friend and I. About Mrs. Lucan."

The old man put on a pair of round wire rimmed glasses and looked at Len. "You are the young man from across the hall. You vant to vhat? Ask questions?"

JB said, "Yes, sir, if you don't mind?"

"You…" He looked JB up and down. "I don't know." He turned slowly and moved into the apartment. "Vell, come in then. And be quick. I don't have much time. At my age, I don't have much time left for anything."

Inside the apartment JB was amazed by the sheer numbers of books that were stacked everywhere. He felt as if they had stepped into a mini branch of the public library. Books filled to overflowing cases that lined three of the walls from floor to ceiling. Books were piled on the floor. Towers of books covered almost every square inch of the room. On the single wall that had no bookcases there were framed degrees and yellowed pictures. Under them was a long table heaped high with more books. In the center of all the books stood a table, a lamp, and a Morris chair.

The Professor sat down in the chair, put his feet on a stack of books he had piled in an ottoman shape, and looked up, perplexity clouding his face. "Vhat is it you vanted to know about Mrs. Lucan?" Then, without waiting for a question, he went on. "She vas a pest. Alvays knocking at my door. Bothering me. Disturbing my reading. Forty years I've bought books to read vhen I retire. Now that's all I do. I did like her cookies though. But if I took them it meant I had to listen to her inane prattle. I got to vhere I just shut the door in her face. But she alvays came back. Vhat are you doing, young man?"

JB turned. "Just admiring your degrees, Professor. From most of the major universities, aren't they?"

"Come closer," he ordered. "My eyesight for distance isn't vhat it used to be. The degrees mean nothing. Several of them are only honorary anyvay. The remnants of a finished career."

JB asked, "You were a paleontologist?"

"One of the top three in this country, young man. It took me forty years to achieve that, and today it means nothing. I vas throvn on the bone pile four years ago. Forced to retire. After heading Fordam's Paleontology department for tventy-five years. But that didn't count for anything. The arschlocher."

"That's German, right? I though I heard a slight accent."

"Yes. I came here in 1934. To escape the madness of Hitler. I vas young then. Only eighteen. I got into a small college right avay. I vas a quick learner, and got my degree by 1939. I got my doctorate three years later."

JB asked, "In 1942? I didn't notice any military pictures on the wall. You weren't in the service during the war?"

Len gave JB a look that questioned why he was letting this old poop prattle on.

"Don't look like that, young man," the Professor said to Len. "Your friend understands the need for an old man's memories. To ansver your question, no, I vasn't in the var. I couldn't fight other Germans could I? Instead, I began to teach. And I vrote. A book on my theory of the extinction of the trilobites. You've heard of them?"

The old man got up and went to one of the bookcases. He bent and pondered over the titles.

Len moved over to JB and softly said, "I skipped a trick and a drink for this?"

JB shushed him.

The Professor returned with a book and showed them a trilobite. It was a crab like creature with multitudes of legs.

"Yuck. No wonder it's extinct," Len said. "Its gross."

"Not to another trilobite," the Professor answered back. His eyes crinkled at his old joke. "So, the book made my reputation. I taught at larger colleges. Then universities. I headed expeditions. I received grants for research, and finally, I had my own department at Fordam. It vas glorious."

"Quite a career, Professor. But earlier you seemed so bitter. Why is that?"

"Not really bitter, young man. Just angry. At time and vhat it does. It saps your body and your mind. It leaves you old, and alone, and useless." The little man seemed to wind down like a toy. He sat in his chair silently.

"Professor, I'm sorry," JB said. "But did you hear or see anything the night Mrs. Lucan was killed?" He looked up blankly. JB repeated the question for him. "No, I heard nothing. I vear a hearing aid." He turned his head to show his ear. "I keep it turned down most of the time."

"And what time..." But JB didn't go on, he realized the old Professor had turned inside himself. He had left them to watch the years passing by as they sped him closer to his final destination. JB motioned to Len and they both left quietly.

"God, that was really depressing," Len said to JB, who was behind him on the stairs to the first floor. He stopped and turned to face him. "If I ever get like that would you please shoot me and put me out of my misery? I'll do the same for you."

"Len, you're like that every time you have a hangover. You should have been shot five years ago."

"Watch it, fella. You've got six months on me, you know. You'll get old before I will."

Len stepped off the stairway into the lobby. A young man, who was standing reading the register of tenants, turned and asked, "Excuse me, but could you tell me where I could find a Mr. Matthews?"

"You found him. What can I do for you?"

"Oh, good. I'm from *Call Masie*. The cleaning service. I'm supposed to clean your apartment."

"What!"

JB grabbed Len's shoulder. "Give me your key!"

Len reached into his pocket and handed the key over.

"I'll meet you upstairs," JB yelled as he rushed up the stairs.

He threw Len's door open and went in. There was no one there.

Len arrived seconds later, the young man following, and said, "Is he here?"

"Nope. The place is empty. And nothing seems to be missing." JB shook his head. "This is weird. Who was that guy?"

"I don't know, Tonto. Did he leave a silver bullet? I'm just damn glad he didn't rob my place. Boy, was that some stupid move or what? I let a complete stranger in here. And I'm sober too." Len turned to the young man. "Do you have any ID?"

The youth handed over a slip of paper from the cleaning service and looked around the studio apartment. "You want me to clean this? It'll take hours."

Len, reading the paper he was handed, said, "Don't worry, most of it goes into the garbage chute. And I tip well. How does an extra twenty sound?"

The boy nodded hesitantly. Len opened the closet door. "The vacuum is in here, supplies are under the sink. The bathroom is through there. And over here is something for me. I'm going to have a drink. JB, do you want one?"

He pulled out a bottle from the cabinet and poured a shot. The boy came out of the bathroom, his face stricken. "Mister, all that stuff on the walls. Is it blood?"

"Yeah," Len said. "I cut myself shaving." The boy took a step back. His eyes widened. "OK, I'll make it an extra forty."

"Make it fifty and you have a deal." Len nodded. The boy bent to get the cleaning gear, and giving Len a wide berth, returned to the bathroom.

"Are you sure you don't want a drink, JB?" He held the glass up to his mouth to swallow.

"No," JB replied. "And neither do you. So put that down."

Len looked at JB. If he had said he was going to strip naked and jump out the window it would have made as much sense. "What for?"

"Well," JB replied. "For one thing, we still have time to get to the rest of the apartments in the building. We have to talk to the tenants. Plus, you can't be in here with him cleaning. You would be in the way. You said so yourself. To the other guy."

"I lied before. This one can work around me. For fifty bucks he should be able to work around the Mormon Tabernacle Choir."

"But I need you, Len. If you're there the tenants will talk. They don't know me. You're a familiar face. Come on, will you? You know how important this is. Unless you want to be charged with a murder rap."

Len downed the shot he had already poured then looked at JB. He had on an expression that made him look like a hired mourner at an Italian funeral.

"Jesus! I'm such a sucker for a man who begs." Len told the cleaning boy where he would be. Then JB led him back down to the first floor.

For a second time JB rang apartment 1-A's buzz-er. When the door finally opened he was con-fronted by a deeply tanned, dark-haired, stunningly built, naked man.

Naked, except for a *Speedo*-style swimsuit he barely wore. The tiny garment did nothing to hide the enormity of his cock and balls, which were bunched like a banana and two plums at his groin. Len looked over JB's shoulder, took a large intake of air, and grabbed JB's arm. JB could almost hear Len pant-ing. He was positive Len's tongue was hanging out.

The naked man's washboard stomach rippled with the movement of his breathing. His waist-size thighs glistened from a slight film of sweat. His biceps bulged when he crossed his arms. Then the muscles on his chest rose and fell as he said, "What-ta' ya want?"

JB smiled. "I'm sorry to disturb you. My friend and I wanted to ask you a few questions, Mr. Terillo. About the death of Mrs. Lucan."

The hunk said, "Who?" His eyes passed back and forth between JB and Len. "I don't know any Mrs....Hey, I know you." He looked at Len. "You live here. Upstairs, right?"

Len, who couldn't take his eyes off the bulk of the man's crotch, nodded dumbly. "So, who's this Mrs. Lucan?" He turned his head back to JB. "Oh, wait. I do know who you mean. The old broad upstairs that killed herself."

"That's the one, Mr. Terillo."

"Call me Johnny." He leaned against the door-jamb and crossed his ankles. This caused both the crotch bulge and his thighs to grow bigger. Len's eyes grew bigger, then crossed.

"All right. Johnny. Except Mrs. Lucan didn't kill herself. It turns out she was murdered."

"No shit." Surprise and concern flew across his face. "Who did it?"

"That's what we're trying to find out."

"So you're talking to everyone in the building, right?" He reached down to adjust his balls. Len's grip on JB's arm got tighter. "I don't think I can help any."

"Any thing you know might help," JB said.

Johnny shook his head. "I only heard about it yesterday evening. When I got back. I've been out of town for the last week."

Len, for some reason, choose this moment to come out of his stupor. He grinned. "On a vacation?" He couldn't have come up with anything more inane.

"You don't vacation in Ohio, mister. I was working."

JB punched Len with his elbow. "Did you know Mrs. Lucan very well?"

"I said I didn't." He looked over at Len. Len's eyes had again strayed downward. "In fact, I knew her about as well as I know him. I just saw her around the building. Listen, is there anymore you want to know? I'm missing the best rays. I have to keep my tan."

"No, I guess not. Thank you for your time."

"No problem." He shut the door on them.

"You can let go now, Len. You're cutting off the circulation in my arm."

"Did you see? That was Johnny Huge. The porn star."

"How could you tell? You never looked at his face."

"I never forget a crotch. My VCR and I have spent many a satisfying hour with him. Do you think he'd let me watch him sunbathe? I promise I would just watch, with maybe some discreet foaming at the mouth."

"And you'd be arrested for loitering with prurient intent."

"But I could be so useful. I could put on his suntan oil. With my tongue."

Exasperated, JB said, "Put your hormones on pause, Len? We have another apartment to talk to."

JB crossed the hall and rang apartment 1-B. There were sounds of coughing and hurried conversation from behind the door. A look of bewilderment appeared on both JB's and Len's faces.

A few moments later the door was opened by a boy in his early twenties. Dressed eclectically, he wore a couple of layers of unpressed shirts, tails out, and a pair of loose baggy trousers with a fly seam that hung around his knees. The legs pooled around his ankles. A pair of patent leather shoes peeked out with silver metal tips on the toes and grosgrain ribbon for laces. The boy's hair stood up in an array of green and pink spikes, and a wispy tail in blue hung at the back. Multiple silver rings on his ears, his nose, his eyebrow, even his lip completed the look. JB also took note that the boy's eyes were spinning in their sockets. The boy said, "What's up stud? Come on in."

He stood aside. A perplexed expression passed between JB and Len as they stepped inside the apartment. The odor of marijuana, freshly smoked, assaulted their senses. On the coffee table was a dust-covered mirror and a razor blade. The dust was colored white and explained the sounds when they rang the bell.

On the couch sat another boy. He was dressed in a similar fashion and was probably more stoned than his friend. At least that would explain his preoccupation with one particular freckle on the top of his hand.

The first young man said, "So, what can I get you sport? We have coke, ludes, and some primo weed. Or ecstasy? How about some black beauties? Red devils, any color of the rainbow. We're having a sale on some great acid." The only thing missing was "Attention, shoppers, blue-light special on aisle seven".

"I think you have us wrong, boys," JB said. "My friend here lives in this building. And we wanted to ask you some questions about Mrs. Lucan. The woman who died on Sunday."

Boy #2 looked up from his freckle. "You mean the rotten old woman who lived upstairs? I heard she died. How did it happen? I hope someone bashed her head in." One of his hands slammed into the other. "Was there lots of blood. I'll bet it was grue-some." He stopped talking then and went back to worrying his freckle.

"Man, you are really out of it," Boy #1 said. He sat on the arm of the couch. "We did hear that she died. What do you want to know about it?"

JB tore his eyes away from Boy #2. "As a mat-ter of fact, she was murdered." The two boys looked at each other. "We were wondering if you might have heard anything that would help our investigation?"

Boy #1 asked, "You a cop?" JB shook his head. "So someone did her in, huh? No, man, we don't know nothing. I think...yeah, we weren't even here that night. We were at the Click. You know, the club. Downtown? We didn't get in until real early. About when..." He turned and tapped Boy #2 on the shoul-der. He looked up. "Hey, noodle nose, when did we get in on Sunday?"

Boy #2 looked at his watch. "At six, I guess. Yeah, that's when."

Boy #1 smiled. "So, you see. We couldn't have heard anything. "

"OK. Did you two know Mrs. Lucan?"

Boy #2 said, "Yeah, but we didn't like her. She's a scummy old broad. She has this really big mouth. And she dressed bad. Real tacky, you know?"

"We knew," Len said.

"She'd always try to get herself in here where she wasn't welcome," Boy #2 continued. "Tried to crash our pad..."

Boy #1 explained. "We had a party one night last month. And she turned up at the door. She had this skanky old feather thing around her neck and kept trying to see who was here. She actually wanted in. We told her to buzz off."

Boy #2 said, "We wouldn't let that old slag heap in here. We couldn't stand her. Especially after she tried to shake..."

Boy #1 snapped, "Shut your face, dork!"

JB, recognizing a subterfuge when he heard one, asked, "What did she try to do?"

Boy #1 answered, "She tried to steal some of our drugs...yeah...we caught her in here once. We hustled her out real fast." Boy #2 nodded his agreement.

Boy #1 reached over and roughly grabbed Boy #2's arm and pulled it toward himself. He twisted the boy's arm until his watch faced upward so he could read it. "Man," he said, "this is a drag. We have a party tonight. You need anymore?"

"No. I guess not. But if you think of anything that might help..."

JB was stopped from saying more by Boy #1 who moved to the door and opened it. As JB and Len walked pass him he said, "Yeah, fer sure." He shut the door. An argument could be heard starting on the other side.

They returned to Len's apartment. The cloying smells of pine, lemon, and various other cleaning fluids filled the air. The place was immaculate. The stacks of newspapers were gone, the dishes were back on the shelves, and the shine on the furniture was almost blinding.

The cleaning boy sat at the table looking much the worse for wear. His hair was plastered to his head from perspiration and large stains were visible under his arms and across his chest.

"Glory, hallelujah, it's a miracle," JB said. "The place is really habitable. Len, you should get down on your knees and kiss that boy's feet."

"A check will be enough," the boy said.

"Right." Len got his checkbook, wrote one out, and handed it over. "Thank you. The place looks terrific."

"You're welcome." The boy wearily put on his jacket. "But do me a favor. Don't ask for me if you call the service again."

"You've got it," Len said, and shut the door on the boy. He turned and headed for the liquor cabinet. "Get yourself a cola if you want, JB. What I want is here."

JB shook his head. Len had spent the whole day trying to get a drink...couldn't wait for the chance... and still wouldn't admit he has a problem with alcohol. But he never would admit to most anything. He always was a master of denial. To look at him you would never guess he was raised in a backwoods Southern town and was ostracized by the other kids as *trash*. That he ran away at fourteen and worked at menial jobs to pay his way to New York and go to acting school. That he dropped a molasses thick accent and created a totally new person from the rubble of his past. What Len couldn't seem to figure out was that he still carried the baggage from those early years inside. To keep away the taunts he still heard, the demons he still saw, was one of the reasons he drank. What he wouldn't admit was that he had to somehow face them or they were going to keep nipping at his ass until the day he died.

JB got his cola and sat at the table. Len had the look of most alcoholics after they got that first drink down. Nerve endings were quieting down, the brain was locking in the proper endorphins, and a satisfied euphoria filled his face. Dope has the same effect on a junkie.

"God, that is good vodka." Len sighed, then he chugalugged the rest of his drink and got up to mix another. "So, what are your conclusions on the tenants, Mr. Mason."

JB brought his mind back to the murder at hand. "Well, Della, its obvious the two druggies weren't telling all they know. I can't see Mrs. Lucan trying to steal drugs. There wasn't a hint of that in her place."

"Besides, she had her collecting to spend her money on. But did you see that one boy? His fantasies could be harmful to another person's health."

"True." JB said. "Though it was probably just the drugs talking. What about the hunk? We only have his word that he was out of town. I mean, why the hell would he go to Ohio? I don't think they have a very big porn industry in the cornbelt."

"He might have just been on location. Playing a farmboy. A very hunky farmboy. I could get into that."

"You just want to get into his *Speedo*. His story could be checked out though. With the airlines. How about the old man? He may not have liked her...and he sure isn't alone in that feeling...but he doesn't strike me as being a killer."

"Unless you consider boring people to death a lethal weapon."

"He's just lonely, Len. All he has are those books, after all those years of work. It's sad I think."

"Yeah, I suppose so. What about Miss Snotty-puss in 4-A?"

JB shook his head. "I don't think so. She's too wrapped up in her own pretensions to do something like this. Murder isn't dignified, you know."

"Isn't that what Claus Von Bulow once said to his lawyer over cocktails? Murder has no class distinctions, JB. How about our refugee from a Universal horror movie in 4-B?"

"That's a real possibility. He was carrying a weapon. Although it isn't illegal to have a gun. But his attitude would give anyone something to think about no matter what."

"All he gave me was the willie's."

"What about Jennifer? She can't be that dumb. If she was she wouldn't be able to function."

"Unfortunately, people like her can. As long as

the rich lover is willing to take care of them."

"Her lover's rich?," JB asked.

"Did you notice the suit she was wearing? One thousand if it's a penny. And the apartment. There's nothing cheap about her or her place."

"So, we have to find out who Andy is, right? We can start on that tomorrow." JB looked at his watch. "Right now I have to get home." He got up and went to the door. As he put his jacket on, he said, "I have a date with Toby."

"You know, just because you're seeing each other doesn't necessarily remove him from the suspect list. He could have murdered her just as easily as any of the others."

"Thanks, Len. That makes me feel real secure." JB opened the door and turned back. "I guess I'll just have to hold on real tight all night so he can't bludgeon me to death."

"You dog!" Len laughed and threw a sugar packet from the bowl on the table at him. JB smiled and shut the door.

The glowing numerals on the digital clock read six fifty-nine A.M. JB was lying in bed on his back, partially awake, Toby's arm across his chest. He was thinking about the night before.

Pepperoni pizza and one hundred and twenty minutes with Bogart and Bacall in *To Have And To Have Not* with Toby beside him. Then quiet conversation between them after the film.

The conversation hadn't started out all cozy

and quiet but had begun on a more accusatory tone. After all Toby was considered a suspect in the murder too.

Sitting on the couch with Toby leaning on his chest, JB had blurted out, "Why are you here, Toby? What do you think you'll get from being here?" He felt Toby stiffen in his arms. "Don't get me wrong, I like spending time with you. But I can't really trust anyone in Len's building. Anyone of you might have done in Mrs. Lucan. And you and I are so different. Hell, I'm almost old enough to be your father."

Toby sat up and looked at JB. "I can only say this again. I had nothing to do with killing Mrs. Lucan. And my being here is more about spending time getting to know you than the murder." Then Toby told JB about his childhood.

There hadn't been a Father around. Only his Mother to look after him. And she worked. That made him a latchkey kid with time to dream of another life, away from the one-horse mentality of his upstate New York hometown.

He always knew he was different from the other kids. He liked other things. Art. Books. Boys instead of girls. Called pretty boy and sissy, among other harsher, cruder, names by his peers, he ended up mostly a loner. That was OK. It gave him time to plan his escape.

It wasn't until high school that he found acting. It allowed him to get away from the confusion's of his life. His good looks even then got him parts and he discovered, much to his own surprise, that he was good. He had talent. His course was set.

He didn't come out until college. An older man, his acting teacher, did the deed, but he wasn't really comfortable with his gayness until he moved to New York City. He found hordes of people like himself and for the first time felt free.

JB then told a few stories from his Kansas past

and they felt themselves grow closer, as if the shar-
ing was a catalyst, a binder, between them. Later
they had made love. It had been slow and passion-
ate. When both were satisfied they lay against each
other and drifted off to sleep.

JB smiled at the memory then decided to try for
at least one more hour's sleep. He wiggled closer to
Toby.

The clock flipped over to seven A.M. and the
phone rang. Toby's head lifted off the pillow. With his
eyes still closed he mumbled, "What?"

"At least he's right on time!" JB leaned over,
kissed Toby on the forehead, and said, "Go back to
sleep." Toby kissed the air and settled back down.
JB got out of bed, grabbed a robe against the morning chill, and went to chew hell of Len for this.

He picked up the phone on the fourth ring. "Len.
For Christ's sake, this is three days in a row..." He
stopped at the voice on the other end of the phone.
"Oh, Lieutenant Kelly. I'm sorry. I thought you were
someone else. What can I do for you?....Well, all
right....Is there anything wrong?....OK....Right....
Good-bye."

JB hung up and stood scratching his head.

An hour later JB was in front of the police station. He had left Toby asleep, a note telling him what
happened on the pillow next to him. JB had no idea
what this was all about, but the tone of Kelly's voice
had left little doubt that JB should haul ass and get
there.

After checking with the on-duty desk sergeant
he went to Kelly's office, knocked, then opened the
door.

Sitting behind the desk, Kelly looked harried and unhappy. So far everything's normal, JB thought. Kelly leaned back in his chair and looked at him sourly. "Sit down, Bent."

He did.

"What the hell are you doing mucking around in my murder investigation?"

So much for a cheery greeting. "I don't understand," JB said.

Kelly shifted in his chair. "At this point we know you've talked to Helmut Lucan, been bumbling around in the dead woman's apartment, and been talking to the other tenants of the building where the main suspect, your friend, lives. God knows what else! Well, I'm here to tell you. Keep the hell out of it! Now do you understand?"

"I get the message, Kelly. But how did you know. Are you having me watched?"

"I know what you've been doing all right. Bent, this is no place for amateurs to be sticking their noses in. So keep out of it. OK? We have an investigation in progress and we'll find out what happened to Sylvia Lucan. We don't need your help."

"Kelly, what you said about Len being the main suspect is what bothers me. I've known him for a lot of years, both sober and otherwise, and I know he didn't kill that woman. He's not capable of it. Besides, what's his motive? From what I can see your investigation won't get you anywhere because you're starting out on a wrong assumption."

"Since when are you an expert on investigative procedure?"

"Kelly, procedure doesn't make room for human beings. You had to have seen what kind of person Len is. He isn't a murderer."

"If that is the case, Bent, we'll find it out. Until then, I've been told to get you out of this. So stay out."

"What do you mean you've been told? Who told you such a thing?"

"My superior. That's who." Kelly looked uncomfortable. "I got called on the carpet this morning, Bent. I don't like being called on the carpet."

"Then your superior was the one who told you what I'd been doing, right?"

"Yeah, so what? All I know is he told me to get you out of this. He said civilians have no place in police matters. And he's right."

"But who told him, Kelly? That's what I wonder."

"Bent, it doesn't matter. What does matter is that if you keep on you're going to be in major trouble."

"All right, Kelly. From here on I keep any investigating I do on a private level."

It was now nine-thirty A.M. JB was at Toby's building. He had returned to his own apartment after his early morning warning and had found it empty. However, Toby had left a note explaining that he needed to get back to his place but to come by for breakfast if he wanted to.

He wanted to. So he rang and was let in through the glass lobby door. Toby stood in the doorway of his apartment. They kissed and walked inside arm and arm.

Len, sitting at the table, looked up from his cup of coffee. "Will you two stop. I can't take this much sweetness and light in my condition."

Len was, it appeared, hungover again. "I didn't know postal services deliver overnight from Tibet," JB said. "Because you look like you were pulled forcibly out of Shangri-La. How you doing, Margo?" He walked over and gave Len a very big, very loud, kiss.

Then rumpled him for good measure.

"Stop that or I'll have you arrested for cruelty to the unwell."

"Speaking of arresting somebody. I spent a most unpleasant half-hour with Kelly this morning. Len, I'm sorry, but you're still the number one suspect in this murder."

"JB, don't try to cheer people up, you're lousy at it. Is that what he wanted to see you about? To tell you I may be going to Sing-Sing soon?"

"No, as a matter of fact, he called me down there to tell me to stay out of their investigation. Although it doesn't look as if they've done very much up to now."

Toby had been putting breakfast together at the kitchen stove. He brought it over and put plates in front of JB and Len. "Enjoy," he said.

"Thanks," JB said. He began to eat. "Try it," he said to Len. "It'll make you feel better."

"I'm much more a brunch person, thank you. I can't stand eggs looking up at me accusingly this early. I can't handle that much guilt before eleven." Len shuddered. "Wait a minute, JB. All you and I did was talk to the tenants. How could that mess up a police investigation?"

"Kelly knew I had talked to Helmut Lucan. So they have probably also talked to him. And he somehow knew we had been in Mrs. Lucan's apartment. Toby, were there any cops here yesterday?"

"Not that I know about." He walked over and sat at the table with them.

"Then how did they know? And I had the impression Kelly got his orders from someone higher up. Whoever that superior was told him about me. The higher up had to have received the information from someone else."

"So, are you going to stop?"

"No way. Kelly's a good cop, but like most cops he can't see beyond the obvious. There's a body in Len's bathtub so Len had to do it. But that solution doesn't answer any of the questions left lying around. And it's railroading Len to boot. I can't let him do that."

Len looked across the table at JB. "Thank you. Really. Anyway, you love playing Miss Marple, don't you?"

"Pick someone else. I look awful in tweed."

"OK. Nancy Drew."

Toby shook his head. "You two have the damnedest relationship. Cutting and slicing with love. What a concept."

JB smiled. "It's word games, Toby. We've been doing it for years. It somehow defines our friendship. You'll find out that when love affairs are over and your real family deserts you, your only choice is to turn to your friends. For many gay people their friends are their families." Len reached across the table and lightly slapped JB's hand. The gesture was both kidding and intimate at the same time. "But, this isn't getting Len out of this mess he's in." JB shook his head to focus. "What we have to do now is try to check out what we were told yesterday. Let's start with the hunk, Johnny Terillo. How do we find out if he really was in Ohio?"

"I know someone who works at a travel agency. He could check out all the flights for Johnny's name," Len said.

"Good idea."

"His number is in my book upstairs. I'll go get it, and bring it right back."

"No, I'll be right up," JB said to Len as he left. "Thanks for breakfast, Toby. And for getting Len up. And, especially for last night."

"You're welcome on all three counts. Is there anything else I can do?"

"You could meet me for dinner."

"You bet. But here. I'll cook."

"Deal," JB said. They kissed. Then JB went upstairs to find Len.

The door had been left standing open. JB took a step inside. It was dark because the drapes hadn't been drawn. JB was about to say something when he spotted Len lying on the floor. He was out cold. JB hurried to him and bent down.

An arm wrapped quickly around his neck from behind. He grabbed at it and tried to pull it away. He was stopped by a hard fist punching into his stomach. Suddenly everything was in black and white. All the color slid away as if melting in the heat of a hot day in August. Another arm covered his eyes and there was only black. A fist hit his stomach again. Then there was a fist to his jaw. Now there was color. Blood red and a sickly shade of yellow. Then the colors sped together to make a putrid sort of orange. A hard object crashed on the back of his neck. Shades of purple and blue were added to the chromatic landscape in his head. The arms holding him upright dropped away and JB crumpled. He fell for what seemed an extraordinarily long time. When he hit the colors started to fade. The show was almost over. He heard a voice that had a foggy sound to it, like a slowed down recording. "Lleett'ss ggeett oouutt ooff hheerree...."

His eyes managed to focus long enough to see a bright flash in front of him. He wondered if his attackers were taking pictures? Or was it the light from the hall striking something? Then it was gone. He shook his head and tried to get up. His arms wobbled and gave out from under him. He landed on the floor again. He lay there as the screen went too black and the movie was over.

It might have been minutes, it might have been hours later when JB finally opened his eyes. The room was still in darkness and Len was still lying on the floor in front of him. He was still out cold.

JB sat up. His hands grabbed his head. Then he heard Toby at the open doorway. "Jesus Christ!," he exclaimed. "What the hell happened?"

JB's head throbbed and his jaw was tender where the intruders had hit him. Even his eyes stung. He shut them against the light Toby switched on. He felt Toby's hands grab his shoulders. "Are you all right," he asked.

JB pointed over at Len. "I'm fine. What about him?"

Toby moved over to Len, bent, and listened. "He's breathing, but he's knocked out." Toby stood and went to the bathroom. He brought back two damp towels. He handed one to JB. He used the other on Len.

JB got up from the floor, sat on the only chair left upright in the room, and looked at the damage.

The cleaning boy had been right to request his not being called again. If he saw this mess he would plotz.

All of his good work had been destroyed. The books were off the shelves; all the cabinets were open and empty. Glassware and bottles had rolled out onto the counter. The light glinted off them drunkenly. The sofa bed was pulled open, its mattress was half on and half off the frame. Every drawer in the apartment had been pulled open, their contents strewn everywhere. Len's clothes had been taken from the closet and were thrown about at random. A single argyle sock dangled off the hanging lamp.

Len, by then, had come to and sat up. He looked around, and burst into tears. Toby held him.

"What is all this?" Toby indicated the mess. "I was on my way to the roof and passed the open door. That's when I found you guys on the floor."

JB shook his head, more to clear it than to answer. "Somebody broke in," he said. "When we interrupted them they used us both for punching bags."

Len wiped his eyes. "But why? I don't have anything worth stealing." He crawled over to a bottle of gin lying on the floor, opened it and took a swig.

"I don't think robbery was what this was about," JB said. "There were two of them and they must have been looking for something."

Len took another gulp from his gin. "But what?"

"Put the bottle down, Len," JB said in an annoyed tone. "You don't need it. And I certainly don't need you drunk right now. We've got to figure this out."

Len kept hold of his bottle but didn't drink again.

JB went on. "This has got to be tied in with the murder. They must have thought you had something in here that would lead to them being arrested. They were scared. At least enough to add assault and battery to their crimes."

"And breaking and entering," Toby said.

JB looked at Len. "That's it!"

Len said, "Then we're only half-criminals, you mean?"

"Right!" JB turned to Toby. "Have you got your keys?," he asked.

Toby pulled out his key ring and held it up.

"Good. Come with me." Toby looked bemused. "Len will explain," JB said. He went out of Len's apartment and up the stairs.

He stopped at the door of 3-B and bent to look at the lock. Len and Toby came up behind him. "It's been jimmied. Try the key, Toby." He stepped aside.

After some effort the key turned in the lock. Toby swung open the door.

Mrs. Lucan's elegant apartment had also been trashed. The paintings were off the walls and the furniture was overturned. The desk drawers stood open and papers were thrown about. It looked as if a rock band had spent the weekend.

"Well, I don't feel so picked on anymore," Len said.

"I don't get it." JB rubbed his sore chin with his hand. "We didn't find anything in here. They...whoever they were, couldn't have either. If the thieves had found anything they wouldn't have hit Len's place." He picked up the Monet from the floor and put it back on the wall.

"They had to have been searching for something specific or they would have taken this. No thief would leave a painting this valuable behind. There has to be something here that incriminates them." He righted a table, picked up the Faberge egg and set it carefully on its stand. Then he sat and stared at it.

Len and Toby began to pick up bits and pieces to put the room back in shape. They had been working only a few moments when JB stood and turned in a circle. He turned with his eyes narrowed.

Len stopped what he is doing. "Are you all right, JB? This really isn't the time for folk dancing, you know?"

"Len, look around. What doesn't fit? You mentioned it the other day."

"You mean that tacky urn? I was right, it doesn't fit. Everything in this room is a treasure, except that."

JB went over to it. It had, probably because of its weight, remained standing. He lifted the lid and reached inside. His arm disappeared up to his elbow. "Nothing."

He pulled his arm out and looked first at the urn and then his arm. "Wait a minute," he said. "This thing is as tall as my arm is long, but I could only reach part way inside." He reached inside the urn again and ran his fingers around.

"Ah. There's a finger hole." He pulled up. "I thought so. This thing has a false bottom. There's something in here."

He pulled out a small leather loose-leaf notebook and handed it to Len. He reached in again and pulled out a key attached to the type of plastic disk hotels use. "These might clear a few things up," he said.

Toby then tapped JB on the shoulder and pointed toward the open door. There was a woman standing in the doorway, looking at the mostly de-stroyed room with a very confused look on her face. JB put the key in his pocket and stood.

The woman was old. Very old. And short. Very short. However, since she was also very thin she looked as if she used to work as a fashion model from Munchkinland. Dressed severely in a dark pinstripe Forties-style suit coat and skirt, she also wore a cream silk blouse with a tightly tied bow at the neck.

She held herself rigidly upright, pushing her shoulders back, doing what she could to disguise the small dowagers hump on her back. Her military stance would indicate the foundation garments from hell were helping her to achieve her wobbly pos-ture. The hair was dark brown, cut in a severe bob at the jawline. Straight bangs covered her forehead and huge thick oval tinted glasses covered and en-larged her squinty eyes. Her make-up, shakily ap-plied, would put her age anywhere between fifty and eighty. Her hands, however, put her somewhere in the late middle.

"May we help you, ma'am?" JB took a step for-ward.

The woman's eyes grew wide for a moment. Then she reached into her shoulder bag and pulled out a slim gold fountain pen and a small notepad. She wrote and held it toward JB. He took it. It read: *Do you sign? I am deaf.* She smiled and held her hand to her ear.

"No ma'am. I'm sorry. I don't." He handed the notepad back, then turned to Len and Toby. "Do ei-ther of you know sign language? She's deaf."

Toby shook his head. Len said, "Only the sign for fuck. I had a deaf trick once and it seemed to be the only sign I needed."

JB turned back to the woman. "I'm sorry. No one here signs. Perhaps between notes and your reading lips we can help you?"

She nodded. JB directed her to a chair, where she sat primly, and began to write.

"Why don't you guys finish getting the place in order while I help the lady."

Len and Toby went to work. JB, once again, turned to the woman. She was holding out her notepad. *I am Lucy Schott. Sylvia's sister. Where is she?*

"Mrs. Lucan's sister?" She nodded. "Ms. Shott. I don't know how to make this any easier, but your sister....is dead." Her hand went to her mouth as she gasped. Then she bent and wrote.

She was murdered? I knew she would be. Who!

"Yes, she was. But we don't know who yet. There are several suspects. How did you know she would be murdered?"

She held up the notepad and jabbed repeatedly at the word *Who!*

"Perhaps the police could fill you in better, Ms. Shott."

She flipped a page and wrote frantically. *My sister was a mean awful woman. Into things not legal. Was it her husband? He hated her!*

"He is one of the suspects, yes, Ms. Schott. Again, you really should talk to the police."

You're not police?

"No. My friend here lives in this building. Someone broke in here. So the two of us and the Super were setting the place in order." She nodded. "I'll give you the name of the officer in charge of the case."

JB turned to look at Len. "Are you about finished?"

"Yeah, just a minute while I check the bedroom."

JB wrote Kelly's name and address on the notepad, then handed it back. "He'll be able to help you. We're about done here. I'm really sorry about your sister. We'll leave you alone so you can have some time to yourself."

She nodded her thanks and then leaned back in her chair Her shoulders dropped and she began to search in her bag for a tissue. Finding one she dabbed at her eyes.

JB, Len and Toby quietly left the apartment leaving the woman to mourn in private.

"Poor old thing. I hid the dirty magazines, JB. So she won't find them right away. The shock of those things could kill her."

"They won't surprise her," JB replied. "She didn't much like her sister either."

"Jeez, did anyone like Mrs. Lucan?" Toby said.

"It doesn't look like it. You know, if she'd been liked by anyone she probably wouldn't have been murdered. As it is we have more suspects than we can handle."

"Well, guys, I have to get back to work. I've got to check the roof for summer damage."

"OK, Toby. And we need to get Len's place back in shape." JB stepped next to Toby. "Will I see you later?"

Toby nodded and headed for the stairs. JB and Len did the same in the opposite direction.

A few minutes later Lucy Schott came out of the apartment and also headed for the stairs. Her face had an unhappy expression as she went down the stairs. With an angry pull she removed the dark wig from her head.

It took them about an hour to get Len's apartment back together. After they finished Len got a drink and JB got himself a cola from the icebox. Len then sat at the kitchen table and leafed through Mrs. Lucan's notebook.

"Well, what did you find?"

Len looked up and handed the book to JB.

"It makes no sense. The woman was loony."

JB examined it. It was a standard square paper notebook with yellow dividers. Each divider had a phrase written on it. Behind those were lined paper with hand-written notes filling them.

"It's got to be a code," JB said. "The dividers are to separate the subjects and the notes refer to them."

"OK. But how do we break the code?"

"Get me a piece of paper." Len found one and handed it to JB. "Thanks." He began to write each of the phrases out of the notebook.

"If I write down each of the headings we might be able to figure this out."

He finished, held it up and looked at it. A second later he set the paper down on the table.

"Well?"

"Nope."

Len picked up the paper.

On it were eight phrases. They read, in order:

Bombay Season	Lord Snowy-White
Winter Vogues	Berlin Assurance
The Pope's Son	Minsky's Cutie
Super Wine	?????????????

"I told you she was crazy," Len said. "The Pope's Son? What the hell is that? How can a Pope have a son?"

"I don't know. But I'm sure this notebook is important to figuring out what Mrs. Lucan had going on. It's got to be what the intruders were looking for."

"Well, the only phrase that makes even a bit of sense is Super Wine. What about the notes?"

"They make about as much sense as the subjects. Here, after Super Wine, it says, and I quote, *No good now. After success can decant.* And after the Pope's Son, it says, *Made confession,* and a date. Bombay Season makes even less sense. *Tour guide arrived. Used roll film. Pictures good.* And a different date.

Behind the question marks she's written nothing."

JB threw the notebook on the table.

"There's no way we can figure out what that means unless we can figure out who the subjects are."

"What about the key?"

"It's from a hotel called The Braxton Arms. On East 79th Street. I suppose it has some meaning. But I don't know what it might be."

"Maybe she has a room there. She mentioned pictures, maybe that's where they are."

"Or in the hotel's safe. I guess we'll have to go over there."

JB stood and got his jacket. Len did the same. "Don't leave the notebook here. Those guys might come back."

JB opened the door, Len grabbed the notebook, and they left the apartment.

The Braxton Arms was a resident hotel that had seen better days. In its heyday it might have been a showplace. Now, many years past its prime, the marble floors were yellowed and the green walls had turned bilious. The lobby's Grand Rapids style furniture sagged from the weight of too many bodies over too long a time. In the stale air hung the smell of many generations of smoke and nicotine.

Behind the scarred wooden desk stood a man who would have looked more at home on down on the docks rather than at an Upper East Side hotel clinging to its last few remnants of gentility. He scrutinized JB and Len while scratching his stomach through his dirty T-shirt. "We don't rent to couples, boys."

"We're not looking for a room." JB said.

"Then what do you want?" A burnt out

cigar stub traveled from one side of his mouth to the other in a continuous journey. Back and forth. Back and forth.

"We found this key. We were wondering who it belonged to. Could you help us?" JB slid the key and a ten dollar bill across the desk.

The clerk picked up the key and the bill. The bill disappeared into his pant's pocket. Then he examined the key. "The tag is ours...at least it was. The key ain't."

"What do you mean?"

He looked over at them as if they were slow. The cigar stopped traveling and pointed straight up. "I mean the key ain't one of ours." The clerk reached behind him and put another room key on the desk. "See. The top of our keys is round. This one's got edges. So it ain't ours. And the tag is one we stopped using about five years ago. This one's pretty beat up too." He pushed their key back across the desk.

JB picked it up. It was in bad shape. Most of the letters had the paint scratched off them. Several of the letters were completely obliterated. JB thanked the clerk and went over to a couch. Len followed behind him.

"What is it?," Len asked.

"Look at this," JB said. "It's a regular key tag. But here, where it should say *Drop in Any Mailbox, Key Will Be Forwarded,* there are scratches through all of the words except Forwarded. Then someone has scratched off the paint on the last part of that word. And look, the top part is gone on the O so it's now a U. After the R the rest is gone. It reads F-U-R."

JB handed the key to Len, went to the desk, and returned with a telephone book. He flipped the pages until he found a number.

"Yeah, look here. The Braxton Furriers. Its address is four blocks away from your place. That's got to be it."

"Come on, Sherlock. What?"

"I'll bet you Mrs. Lucan has a fur stored at this place. And this is the key to a locker. And what would you bet there isn't something else stored there too?"

"But, JB. The whole tag is scratched up. And Fur isn't the only letters that are scratched off. Look." Len held out the key.

The D and the p from Drop, The y from Any, The M and the X from Mailbox, and the K from Key were also left on the tag besides the Fur of Forwarded. The rest of the letters were all scratched away and missing.

"The bottom one's are the only one's that spell anything. The rest is gibberish."

"That's my point, JB. This might be an old tag she used so she wouldn't lose the key."

"But it fits. The word FUR is on it and there's a Braxton Furriers." Len looked doubtful. "Well, the easiest way to find out if I'm right is to call." JB got up and went to the phone booth. He made his call and walked back to Len.

"There's good news and there's bad news."

"I could use the good."

"OK. Mrs. Lucan does have a coat at the Braxton Furriers."

"And?"

"And, she's the only one who can get it out. They have an electronic security system that requires a special code to allow access to the storage area. Without the code we can't get in. I even told the clerk I was her nephew and she asked me to get it for her. No good. She has to use the code to get the fur."

"Damn. What do we do now?"

"We could start by finding the code." JB started walking toward the outside.

"JB, what good will finding the code do? You said she has to use it."

"Well, Len, we have to start someplace."

L ike Alice down the White Rabbit's burrow JB shouted for Toby at the stairwell next to his apartment. He hadn't answered his doorbell and the open door to the basement led them to believe he might be down there.

A shout from somewhere in the depths proved them right. JB and Len picked their way down the steps and along a hallway toward a light at the end.

Toby stood next to a washing machine in a concrete bunker type room. A basket of clothes sat at his feet. "Hi guys. Where did you disappear to? I went back to Len's place and no one was there."

"We had an errand to run. Toby. I was wondering if we could have Mrs. Lucan's key again?"

He pulled out his key ring. "Sure. What's up?"
He handed the key over. "Wait. What about her sister?"

"We'll use this only if she's not there. There's
something we have to find in her place. I'll get this
back to you." JB looked around. "Len, where are
you?"

His voice came from a distance. "Over here. In
the next room."

JB went to the hall and over to where the voice
came from. Toby followed. "What are you doing?" He
stopped. "What's all this?," he said.

The room was large and ran the full length of
the basement. In it was a series of wire cages filled
with trunks and other bric-a-brac. Toby came into
the room behind JB and said, "Storage. For the tenants. One space for each apartment."

Len was inside the space marked 2-B surrounded by suitcases and boxes. A trunk was open
in front of him. "I wondered where this was." He held
up a ratty looking raccoon coat.

JB shook his head. "It's totally amazing to me
the kind of junk people accumulate. What the hell is
that?"

"It's from a production of *The Boyfriend*. I
did it in repertory with *Charley's Aunt* ages ago." He
slipped on the coat. "Whack-a-doo, whack-a-doo," he
sang as his arms flapped in the air.

"Put it away, Toots. We have work to do." JB
turned to Toby. "I'll give you the key back at dinner.
Will that be all right?"

"I need to talk to you about that." Toby moved out
into the hall. JB followed. "JB, I have to call off dinner tonight. My da....I mean, my boss called and he
wants me to have dinner with him. I hope you don't

mind?"

"No. It's OK. It's your job after all. I mean I'm disappointed, but I understand."

Len called from the stairway. "Are you ready?"

"Sure. I'll be right there," JB shouted in Len's direction. Then he turned to Toby. "We'll talk tomorrow. OK?" He started to walk away. Toby stepped after him and touched his shoulder. JB turned back to face him.

"I really am sorry." Toby stepped close and hugged JB. Then he kissed him on the cheek. "I'll call you tonight. I promise."

JB nodded and went up the stairs.

"What's wrong, JB You two have an argument already?"

JB, after knocking on Mrs. Lucan's door, put the key in the lock. "No. Toby had to cancel dinner. He has to meet his boss tonight. At least that's what he said."

"But you're not so sure?"

He turned the key and opened the door. "Right. I think he has to meet someone but it might not be his boss." He walked to the desk. "Well, this is the most likely place to start." He opened a drawer and then looked back at Len.

He was standing in the center of the room, his mouth opened, his eyes wide. JB shut the drawer and went to him. "What's wrong? You look lik..."

Len shook his head and pointed toward the wall. JB turned. "Jesus, it's gone!"

Len whispered, "The sister?"

Neither of them heard the bedroom door open, or saw the man step into the room. The man said, "What's gone, boys?"

Len shouted and clutched at JB. JB sighed, then

peeled Len's arms from around him. He looked over at the figure in the doorway. "Kelly, what are you doing here?"

"I might ask you the same thing, Bent. What the hell are you doing here? I remember that I specifically told you to keep away from this murder investigation. That was you I talked to, right? And that was only this morning, wasn't it? Well?"

"Yes," JB said, his eyes cast downward.

"All right. Then do you want to explain your being here or should I just assume you didn't give a fiddlers damn about what I said?"

JB said nothing, but stood with a look of penitence that Joan of Arc could have used during her trial.

"I am going to guess that your silence is meant to answer my question. You realize I can have you both hauled in for tampering with a crime scene? So, to keep me from doing that, you sure as hell better tell me what you meant by 'it's gone' real fast."

"There was a small painting on the wall. It was here earlier, now it's missing."

"What kind of painting?"

"What do you mean?"

Kelly was annoyed. "I mean was it a print or an original? Was it contemporary or an old master? The victim had a pretty expensive taste for antiques."

"It was a Monet," Len said. "An original Monet."

"What?"

"That's what Len thinks, Kelly. I'm not so sure. Mrs. Lucan's stuff is valuable, sure, but a real Monet is worth way more than any of this could ever be. It's priceless."

"Not priceless exactly," Kelly said. "But way more than Sylvia Lucan could have afforded. Why would you think her painting was original, Mr. Matthews?"

"Well, the style was right. The subject matter

was right. Even the coloring and technique was right. And it was signed. Monet. Right on the bottom."

Kelly interrupted. "You say it was signed Monet?"

Len answered, "Yes."

Kelly said, "Then it was probably a fake. Claude Monet always used his full name to sign his works. He didn't just use a surname."

Kelly sat on the couch and was silent. He was searching through the files of his mind. "Years ago, the Nazis had a booming business going. During the war they traded in forged masters. And there was usually some mistake on the copy. That was their out. It wasn't really a fake if there was an obvious error. So anyone with some knowledge of art history would know it was bogus. There was a wrong date, or an incorrect signature. Problem was that many art collectors were not knowledgeable and many of those fakes ended up being sold as originals. A few years ago Helmut Lucan was supposed to have acquired several of those paintings and was selling them as originals. When it was investigated nothing was found. There wasn't any evidence. But our murder victim was his ex-wife and now seems to have had one of what he was accused of selling. That would be quite an ax to hold over someone's head, wouldn't it?"

JB looked at Kelly. "You mean she might have been holding the painting for some sort of ransom? And he got tired of waiting for her to return it. So he came after it..." He paused for emphasis. "...and killed her to get out from under the threat of exposure she represented."

"I mean it enough to talk to Mr. Lucan again."

"Can we come along?"

"I'm not crazy about the idea of you two tagging along, but I'm going to need you to identify the painting. If it's there. But after this, I want your promise you'll stay out of this."

"If you're right about him having the forgery that means Len's no longer a suspect. I'll have no reason to be in it."

Kelly pulled a roll of yellow plastic tape from his pocket. "Let me get this apartment sealed and we'll find out if I can get you off my neck and close this murder case at the same time."

The officious young man that acted as Helmut Lucan's assistant was as nervous as an apricot poodle nipping at the heels of Kelly, Len, and JB. His mission in life seemed to be to keep them from entering his boss's office.

"You can't go in there. Mr. Lucan is in conference," he snipped. "I have strict orders not to let anyone in."

"Young man," Kelly said. His height and bulk outdistanced the man by six inches and more than a hundred pounds. He loomed over him like a gargoyle on a cathedral. "I am from the New York City Police. If you want to try and stop me from going in there you had better have a judge in your pocket and plenty of insurance. Because you'll need them both."

Kelly raised a ham-like fist. It was about the same size as the assistant's head, although not nearly as well groomed.

The assistant's face went white. He stepped aside, loyalty to one's employer not being a priority when faced with the prospect of major plastic surgery.

"Police brutality," JB said to Len from behind Kelly's back.

"Sometimes action speaks louder that a warrant, Bent." Kelly put his hand on Lucan's door and gave it a shove. It slammed open without protest.

The frosted glass-walled room stood empty, but JB noticed a door on the other side just clicking shut.

"Through there, Kelly." JB pointed a finger.

Kelly took off for the door as if he were again on the football field. He had the ball. He was going for the winning down.

Len put a hand on the assistant's shoulder. "Don't you worry, sweetie. You did the right thing. Even Dian Fossey had enough sense not to argue with a gorilla."

Kelly slammed against the door on the other side of the cubical with his shoulder. It slipped its lock and opened with a loud splintering noise. As the doorknob hit the wall behind it the frosted glass disintegrated into chunks of knife like pointed icicles and crashed to the floor.

"You know, just when we think we have him housebroken, he pulls something like this." JB shook his head.

Kelly could be heard shouting in the next room. "Hold it, Lucan. You don't want to do that."

JB and Len ran across the office and into the back storeroom. Kelly was standing with his revolver held out in both hands. It was aimed at Helmut Lucan.

Lucan stood at a worktable. His hand was holding a knife to a painting. It was lying on the table with a slash running from corner to corner, ruined. Lucan's face had the look of a trapped animal, all growl and bluster, but he knew the jig was up.

"Put the weapon down, Lucan. I don't want to have to shoot. Bent, get the painting."

The knife clattered from Lucan's hand as JB moved cautiously toward the table. He reached over and slid the painting to his side, at the same time he moved the dropped knife away from Lucan's reach.

"This is it, Kelly. The picture from Mrs. Lucan's apartment."

"God damn that woman," Lucan cursed. "Even when she's dead she causes me nothing but trouble."

"Can you put these on him, Matthews?" Kelly was holding out a pair of handcuffs.

"Can Bette Midler shake her tits?"

Len took the cuffs and in seconds had Lucan's arms behind his back with the cuffs snapped on his wrists. "Not too tight are they, honey?" Len looked at JB. "Sorry, force of habit."

"Mr. Lucan, you have the right to remain silent..."

"Wait a minute. I'm being arrested? For cutting a painting? In my own art gallery?"

JB said, "More likely for stealing another persons property. Mrs. Lucan's things belong to her sister now."

"Sister? Sylvia had no family. She was an only child. They had her, saw what they had done, and couldn't bear to bring another into the world. And both her parents are dead."

Len's mouth opened. JB shook his head. Len's mouth closed.

"Mr. Lucan, you're going to be booked for committing the murder of your ex-wife." Kelly prepared to start the Miranda again.

"But that's crazy. I didn't kill Sylvia."

"Tell me about it at the station." Kelly grabbed Lucan's shoulder and started walking him toward the doorway. The assistant, who had been standing all this time with his hand to his mouth, stepped out of the way.

Len leaned over to him and softly said, "Tell me. Sweetie. Do you own a dark page boy wig?"

Kelly could be heard reading the whole Miranda as he headed Lucan to the gallery's front door.

After Kelly had carted Lucan off to the station, Len turned to JB.

"If Mrs. Lucan doesn't have a sister, then who

was that woman in her apartment this morning? If you want my opinion, I think it was the assistant in drag."

"Come on, Len, either one of us could clock a drag from twenty feet away. That was a woman this morning. Anyway, the assistant is way to young."

"You'd be amazed what you can do with a little Max Factor and some *Silly Putty.*"

"Len, I was less than three feet away from her. Believe me, it was a real woman. And, I think she was the real killer."

"But the lieutenant just arrested Lucan for it."

"I know. I think he's wrong."

"But Lucan has a motive."

"So does everyone else we suspect." JB went on, "If that woman wasn't the real murderer she, at least, knows who it really was. She was trying to misdirect us toward Lucan to take the heat off herself, or whoever really killed Sylvia Lucan."

"If that's true it means it isn't over. I could still be arrested."

"It means Kelly won't pursue this again until Lucan is proven innocent. So we have a little time to ourselves. Which I could use. I have some of my own work to do."

"But, JB, I..."

"Len, stop. We'll start again tomorrow. OK?"

Len had seen JB's *Go away...I need some solitude* expression before. "Uh, sure, OK, I'll call." Len said. They hugged and Len walked away.

JB, after stopping at his local electronics store to make a purchase, carried the box home, spent an hour puttering needlessly around the apartment, and finally, with nothing else to do, pulled dinner from the freezer.

That Toby had canceled their evening together bothered JB more that he wanted to admit. I suppose, he thought, I'll have to accept that he has other people in his life. But why would he not be truthful about it? It was obvious he had someone other than his boss to meet. Probably an old boyfriend. Anybody as young as Toby was sure to have a whole bunch of young and good-looking studs after him.

Realizing that this kind of thinking led only to pulling out old Billy Holiday records and feeling sorry for himself, JB turned on his word processor and tried to really get some work done. But somehow the crime George did to Martha didn't grab his attention tonight. The murder of Sylvia Lucan kept interrupting as if it were a child asking *Why?* And asking it again and again.

With Helmut Lucan arrested it meant Len was off the hook, but that was trading one innocent man for another. Lucan couldn't have killed her. It just didn't add up. JB pondered the facts he had so far and all he got was more questions.

Why wouldn't Lucan have taken the painting the same night he killed the woman? Why would he wait two days? And why was the so-called sister trying to direct us to thinking Lucan was the killer? The only conclusion possible was the same one as before. Lucan didn't do it. It was more likely the sister, whoever she was?

It wasn't Mrs. Forsyth-Peal. The weight alone ruled her out. Could it be Jennifer? Len said makeup could do amazing things and she was supposed to be an actress. Or was it someone else? One thing was for certain, that was not a man dressed in a skirt and heels. As unlikely as it seemed, maybe Sylvia Lucan did have one lone friend in this world. And her friend thought that Helmut Lucan killed his ex-wife. But he didn't do it. JB found himself right back where be began. He leaned back in his chair, frustration clouded his thinking processes.

Writing was impossible without concentration, so he got up, turned off the processor, and then turned on the TV planning to lose himself in an hour or two of mindless sitcoms. After fifteen minutes of flat jokes and canned laughter he turned off the TV and went to bed. When he settled he picked up a dog-eared copy of *The Maltese Falcon*. After about five pages his head drooped and he was asleep.

When the phone rang at seven A.M., for the fourth morning in a row, JB woke up about half way. He smiled to himself, plumped his pillow and said, "This'll fix em." Then he fell back into a contented sleep.

What the caller got, after the fifth ring, was JB's newly purchased answering machine saying: *JB here. If you're calling before nine A.M., I'm asleep. If you're calling after ten P.M., I'm working. Anytime in between, I'm not home. Leave a message...*beep.

The machine worked twice that morning. The second time JB didn't even wake up.

JB had an internal wake-up service. He told himself, as he fell asleep, when he wanted to get up and the next morning within ten minutes either side of the given hour he was awake.

At nine A.M. he crawled out of bed. He put a teabag into a cup of water and put both into the microwave. He waited the few seconds necessary for nuking, then gulped the brew. There wasn't an Englishman alive who would approve of this method of making tea, but it served to get that first jolt of caffeine coursing through the body. Besides when barely awake it was about all that JB could handle.

The liquid revived him enough to switch on the radio and let the world in for the day. Where he usually got music, this morning he got the tail end of the hourly newscast.

A terminally peppy announcer's voice said, "...with no clouds and temperatures in the mid-sixties. It's a beautiful day outside New Yorkers. To recap the mornings headlines..."

As JB reached over to turn the radio off—He wasn't really ready for the world after all—the announcer said a familiar name.

"Helmut Lucan, prominent New Yorker and Madison Avenue art dealer, was released from police custody this morning. He was being questioned regarding the death, three days ago, of his ex-wife Sylvia Luc..."

That meant one of two things, JB thought. Either Lucan had a very good lawyer or he was no longer a suspect. If it was the latter that put Len back at the top of Kelly's possible list. It also put figuring out who really had done it as the number one priority for the day.

He went to check the two messages on the answering machine. The first one was from Len, telling him what he had just heard on the radio. The second was from Lieutenant Kelly. He was asking JB to meet him for lunch at a deli on Third Avenue in the thirties. And would he bring his friend, Matthews, along with him.

That last part didn't set well with JB. Why would Kelly need to see them both? Unless it was to tell them what he already suspected.

He dialed Len's number. When he picked up, JB said, "Len, I've heard the news...Right, it doesn't sound terrific... But, we still know a few things the police don't, even if we haven't figured them out yet.... So, we're back looking for the code for her fur.... OK?....Oh, I got a call from Kelly this morning....He wants us to meet him...." JB told Len where the place was and what time to be there, then hung up.

He rolled the tape back and re-set the machine to answer.

As he went to the bathroom to shower he realized he hadn't heard from Toby. Humm? Why hadn't he called?

"Pastrami on rye...on the lean side, please...and lots of mustard," JB told the deli man behind the counter. He could see Kelly sitting in the back booth under a sign announcing that the establishment ran a kosher kitchen.

He waved to the Lieutenant, who acknowledged him with a delusory wave of his hand. Then Kelly went back to spooning chicken noodle soup into his mouth from the large bowl in front of him. JB walked to the back and slid into the seat across from the as usual dour faced policeman.

"You know, Kelly, I always heard the Irish were a happy people. You're sure not one of them. What happened to you?"

"You ever hear of the Black Irish? They were referring to their moods. Where's Matthews? I wanted both of you here."

A waitress set down the sandwich JB had ordered. He slathered on more mustard from the jar on the table. "He should be here soon. Are we here to talk about Lucan being released? You're not going to try to scare Len with prison again are you?"

"No more questions. I'll tell you both when Matthews is here. I don't want to have to say it twice."

"All right, but please, Kelly, don't get too rough on him. He tries to cover it with jokes but he's pretty scared. His life hasn't been going so great the last few years and this could just about finish him..."

Right then Len walked in the door and straight back to the booth. Following behind him was Toby. "Hi, Lieutenant. Hi, JB. Look what I found hanging around the lobby of my building." He put his arm across Toby's shoulders and pulled him close. "When I was a kid I was always dragging home stray puppies. Now that I'm older I drag along stray men. Lieutenant, you know Toby Gallo, don't you?" The two men slid in next to JB.

JB laced his fingers and set them on the table. "All right," he said. "We're here now. What did you want to say Kelly?"

"I wanted to tell you about Lucan for one thing. We let him go this morning because he had an airtight alibi. With witnesses. He was with someone all night so he couldn't have killed his ex-wife. But that won't be the end of his case. We turned his file over to the district attorney's office to investigate his selling fakes as originals through his gallery. He took the painting from the victim's apartment because it would have incriminated him. As we guessed she was using the painting to extort money from him. She had taken several other fake paintings from him at the time of the divorce and had been selling them back to him one by one. That is until last year. Lucan said she suddenly decided to keep the last painting. She said she liked it and didn't need his money anymore."

Kelly leaned back in the booth. This was the part that irked the hell out of him. Complimenting people for doing something they weren't supposed to be doing in the first place.

"Also, on orders, I have to say thank you. You both helped the department to catch Lucan. He'll probably spend jail time for fraud. Without you two we wouldn't have found evidence to convict. Next, I want to warn you again about staying the hell out of this investigation. The Chief is pissed that you were in her apartment. If you guys get caught messing in this again I'll have to throw the book at you. That's it. That's all I have to say."

Kelly had recited the majority of his speech as if he were doing a Jack Webb as Sergeant Joe Friday impression. He looked at his watch. "I have to get back to work." He got up from the booth. Grabbing JB's check, he said, "This is on me. Listen, I know what I just said won't mean diddly to either of you. So be careful. And if you do find out anything, call me. I don't want another homicide along with the one I already have." He walked to the cashier.

"Well, that wasn't so bad," Len said. "I think I understand why you like him, JB." Len took half of JB's sandwich and moved to the other side of the booth.

"Yeah, I do like the guy..."

Len made a face. "God, this sandwich is dry. I need something to wash it down. I'll be back." Len went to the counter, leaving Toby and JB together.

"JB, I know I should have called this morning. But I didn't know what to say. I'm sorry about last night."

"You don't have to apologize again, Toby. I know you have a life of your own."

"I did have to see the owner of the building, JB. And I got in really late, or I would have called."

"Toby, how about you and I start over. OK?" JB took Toby's hand in his.

Toby said, smiling. "Would you like to come for dinner tonight?"

JB pulled Toby's palm to his lips and gently kissed it.

"That would be lovely."

Toby took his hand from JB's, then traced his finger along JB's jaw, then held his finger at JB's lip for a long moment. They sat looking at each other, saying nothing and still saying everything that needed to be said.

"I see you two are being disgustingly affectionate again." Len put three glasses of seltzer water on the table and slid into the booth.

JB straightened up. "OK, Len Just for you we'll stop. So, let's get back to the case at hand?"

Len said, "Not at all what I had in mind. You do know how to poop a party don't you?"

Toby said, "Actually, it's not such a bad idea. My boss is really upset about this murder in his building. The quicker it gets solved the quicker he's off my back."

"I see. You're both ganging up on me." Len sipped his drink. "All right. Then how are we going to find the code to Mrs. Lucan's fur?"

Toby said, "Well, we can't go to the apartment anymore. It's sealed."

JB shook his head. "I don't think the code is in the apartment anyway. We searched it pretty well and there wasn't anything we found that resembled anything like it. It must be someplace else."

"But where," Len asked.

"Toby, answer me a question. Does Mrs. Lucan have a storage bin in the basement?"

"Yeah, but there isn't much in it. Just a few boxes and a trunk and some other junk."

"Well, all we're looking for is a card with numbers on it. OK, men, it's once more down into the depths."

Toby broke the dime store lock on Mrs. Lucan's storage bin with a piece of pipe he found on the basement floor. Inside were three cardboard boxes, each filled with chipped dinnerware and a couple of old figurines, none of which had any great value.

What was of most interest was an old trunk. The men decided to take it up to Len's apartment to open and check out the contents. The trunk, reminiscent of a military footlocker, was locked and had a heavy feel when JB tried to lift it.

"Give me a hand with this will you?" JB hefted

one end of the rectangular box.

"Do I look like a beast of burden?," Len groused.

"No, you look like a pain in the ass."

"If I lift that trunk it won't be my ass that's pained. It'll be my back."

Toby picked up the other end. "I'll do it," he said.

"Thanks, Toby," JB said. "With you helping I won't have to listen to Len moan and groan all the way to the second floor."

"If I remember correctly, you used to love hearing me moan and groan."

The end of the trunk JB held dropped to the floor. "That's it, Len," he shouted. "You've gone to far. You never know when to stop, do you? You always have to take the banter one step over the line. You are really such a bitch."

Len's eyes narrowed. "That may well be, but there's always a grain of truth in it. I'm an honest bitch."

"They don't give gold stars for mean and vicious, Len. Christ, you could open envelopes with that tongue of yours."

Len's face turned pink. JB braced himself for a tirade of monumental proportions. But, instead of coming up with a retort, Len turned on his heel, then loudly stomped out of the bin and up the basement stairs.

"Is he going to be all right?"

"Oh, sure. He'll sulk for about fifteen minutes or so and then everything will be fine. What he doesn't understand is why people are still angry with him when he's already forgotten the whole thing. It used to drive me crazy."

They lifted each end of the trunk and maneuvered it out of the bin. Then they took it up the two flights of stairs to Len's apartment.

The door stood open. Len sat at his desk nursing his wounded feelings with a glass of vodka. When JB and Toby came in he turned away and refused to look at them.

JB, after they put the trunk down, asked Toby to find a screwdriver in the hall closet. Then he went over to Len.

"Len, I'm sorry. I just felt that what you said was inappropriate in front of Toby. If I hurt you, I really am sorry."

"Here's the screwdriver," Toby said.

JB went back and they both got down on their knees to break the lock on the trunk. Len stayed at the desk, not saying anything, and played with the key they had found in Mrs. Lucan's apartment.

Len heard JB and Toby lifting the lid on the trunk. Then Toby said, "It's just a bunch of old clothes and stuff."

"Well, check the pockets and the handbags. The card might be in one of those,"

"What's on this card anyway?"

"The guy at the fur salon said it was a six-digit combination code, whatever that is. Just look for something that has numbers on it."

Len sat staring at the keytag in his hand. After a moment he pulled the phone over to him, then reached into a desk drawer and pulled out pencil and paper. Looking back and forth between the paper and the phone he wrote furiously. When he was done he said in a small voice, "JB."

JB didn't answer. So Len said it again only louder, "JB."

"What? Did you say something, Len?"

"Did you know that you could play *Mary Had A Little Lamb* on the telephone?"

"What? No, I didn't know that. Thank you for that illuminating piece of information."

"JB, I'm not crazy. Musical notes have letters. *Mary Had A Little Lamb* is E-D-C-D-E-E-E. That translates to 323-3333."

"OK. I'll bite. What does that have to do with anything?"

"Do you remember Mrs. Lucan's keytag? It spelled Fur, right? Then there were other letters still visible. Not every letter was scratched off. You said it was gibberish."

By this time JB and Toby had moved over behind Len.

"Well, if you take the letters still showing on the tag. D-p-y-M-x-K. And compare them to the letters on the phone you get 379695. That's six digits isn't it?"

JB slapped Len on the back. "I think I'm going to start calling you Sam Spade. That's it, Len. You've found the code!" JB bent down and hugged him.

Len grinned. Then he took on a puzzled expression. "Just one thing, JB. Now that we have what we think is the code, how are we supposed to get the fur? This isn't *The Dead Walk At Midnight,* you know?"

"He's right, JB. Without Mrs. Lucan the code does us no good," Toby said.

"Damn!"

JB moved away from the desk and returned to Mrs. Lucan's trunk. Kneeling, he started to fold and put her clothes neatly back inside the trunk. A minute later he started pulling things out again.

Len asked, "What are you doing?"

JB sat back. He was holding a Lucy orange wig in his hand. He looked over at Len. "Didn't you say you once played in a production of *Charley's Aunt*?"

"In short, this has got to be one of the most harebrained ideas I've ever heard!" Len turned and went back into the bathroom.

Toby sat at the table with his hands over his

mouth trying to keep his fits of laughter held in. JB, sitting across from him, shouted to Len, "Just get done, all right. And check your eyebrows. I think one was higher than the other one." Toby stifled another giggle.

A few minutes later JB said, "Are you about ready, Len? It's almost three and the place closes at five."

"If this crazy idea is going to work at all it has to be done right. Hold your horses."

"Oh, for Christ's sake, we're not going to tea dance at the Plaza, you know?"

Toby began to snicker again. He stopped when Len appeared. "Good Lord," he said. "You know, this just might work."

JB started to applaud.

Len stood in the doorway in full drag. Three pairs of hose, two white and a black lace pair, covered the hair on his legs. Articles from Mrs. Lucan's trunk constituted his clothing. He wore a chiffon dress with a flounced neckline and long sleeves. Len had pushed these up to hide the fact they weren't quite long enough. The dress was printed with large poppies in orange and red on a full gathered skirt that hit Len just above the knees. On both wrists were several bracelets and on his fingers were stick-on nails painted red. He wore pad's—pillows from the sofa—at the hips and rear, socks filled with rice for his breasts. This all served to match the shape of the woman in the pictures they had found in the trunk. On Len's head, now combed and fluffy, was the wig JB had pulled out earlier.

Using the same pictures as his guide, Len's make-up was probably more theatrical than was usual for street wear. It was necessary since he had added lines, wrinkles and eye-bags to make himself appear the lady's age...about sixty.

Covering the top of the wig was a red hat with black feathers and heavy popcorn netting over the face. The net diffused Len's features and softened the heavy make-up. It also made him almost a dead ringer for Mrs. Sylvia Lucan.

"Damn, Len! You really do look like her," JB said awed by the tranformation.

"You mean I look like an overage hooker after taking on the Seventh Fleet!"

"Well, not the whole Seventh Fleet—maybe just a platoon. But, honestly, you do look like her."

"He's right," Toby said. "You really do look very good. You're taller, but the resemblance is pretty spooky."

"Great. If I'm ever hard up for money I can always join a road company of *La Cage Aux Folles*. We're never going to get away with this, JB."

"I don't know why not. I'll do all the talking, OK? You just nod a lot. People see what they expect to see. You look enough like Mrs. Lucan that they'll see Mrs. Lucan. It's not like we're trying to fool her mother, for God's sake. These people see her, at most, three times a year."

"What if the numbers aren't right? What then?"

"Then I'll make some excuse and we'll leave." JB looked at his watch. "Come on, Len. It's getting late."

Len slipped into low-heeled shoes and picked up a handbag with the plastic tag and key inside.

Out on the sidewalk JB began to walk toward Third Avenue. Len stayed standing where he was. "If you think I'm going to walk the streets of New York, in broad daylight, dressed like this, you're crazy. Besides, a lady never walks when she can ride. Get a cab."

"Getting a bit too much into the part, aren't we?" Len continued to glare.

"All right. I'll be back in a moment." JB walked off toward Lex mumbling to himself about method actors.

The cab driver didn't even blink when he pulled up and Len got into the car with JB. In New York a cabby was used to seeing almost everything.

While he drove them to the fur salon he regaled them with a story about a fare and her orangutan he delivered to the Algonquin Hotel the week before.

At the salon Len got out and sailed inside ahead of JB, who had to pay the driver. He began to make change but when JB saw what Len had done he told him "Forget it," jumped out, and rushed for the salon door.

JB got inside just in time to see Len hold out his hand to a simpering bald man in his fifties. The man bowed, kissed the offered hand, and said, "It's so good to see you again, Madam Lucan. What am I able to do for you?" Len's head turned back and forth looking for JB. The movement caused the feathers on his hat to bob and weave erratically.

JB sidled up beside Len. "My Aunt Sylvia is quiet all right, thank you. I believe I spoke with you earlier?" The man acquiesced. "Good. Then, as I told you, Mrs. Lucan would like to check on her coat.

Len nodded at the man. His feathers bobbed gaily. The man immediately bowed again, gestured and preceded them as they walked toward the rear of the salon. He opened a mirrored door and stepped aside. His hand indicated what looked like a tele-phone touch-tone dial. Above it were six little flash-ing red lights.

Len reached into his handbag, extracted the key and stepped up to the keyboard. He took a deep breath and slowly punched in the six numbers.

The red lights stopped flashing, remained static while neither JB or Len took a breath, and then all turned green at once. When nothing happened JB said, "What's wrong?"

The man turned around from having his back to them and looked at the lights. "The system is waiting for the second half of the sequence. As I told you, it's a combination code." He turned away again.

Len's feathers were moving as if they were caught in a hurricane. He looked at JB, panic on his face, and mouthed the words, *What will we do?*

JB shrugged and shook his head. Finally he said, "I'm sorry. My Aunt can't seem to remember the second part of the code. We'll have to return another time."

JB reached for Len's arm and the bald man started to clear the keyboard. A few steps away Len shouted, "Crips!" in his best basso voice. He turned, stepped up to the shop assistant, tapped him on the shoulder and waved him away.

"She has a touch of bronchitis," JB explained to the now wide-eyed assistant.

Len again slowly punched in the six numbers. The lights again stopped flashing and turned green. Then Len quickly punched another six numbers. He shut his eyes and crossed his fingers.

"Jackpot!" JB exclaimed. The green lights were flashing in sequence as the door clicked open slightly. The assistant grabbed the door handle, pulled, told them to take their time inside, and then pushed it closed when JB and Len had entered.

"What did you use for the second sequence?"

"I used her name. Sylvia. If the letters on the tag were numbers why not her name too? It seemed logical."

"Well, thank God it worked."

JB and Len looked around the vault. The room felt cold, but dry, and was lit with two huge crystal chandeliers. In the center of the carpeted floor stood a velvet red round tufted settee. On both sides were rows of tall pink painted lockers, each with a brass number on its front.

They checked the tag, which was numbered 142, and began to look at each locker. Finally JB said, "Here it is."

Len came over, inserted the key and opened the door. Inside, on a satin padded hanger, hang a full length, long sleeved white chinchilla coat. Len gasped. Then he reached in and pulled the coat out.

Walking to the far end of the room where there was a floor to ceiling mirror, he put the coat on and twirled. "It's magnificent!" he purred. Then he struck a pose, with one leg out, and looked again into the mirror. "I do look good in fur, don't you think?" He turned to see another angle. "And this is definitely my color. Then again, a pinker shade would better compliment my hair."

"Len, get a grip. We're here to find clues, remember?" JB checked the inside of the locker. "There's nothing here. It must be in the coat. We'll have to check it."

Reluctantly Len took the coat off and laid it on the settee. JB checked the inside and outside pockets, than began to check the sleeves.

"Just what are we looking for, JB?"

"I'm not sure. Anything unusual." He started running his hand along the bottom of the coat. He stopped. "Now, here's something odd. There's something sewn into the lining here." He flipped the coat over and using the locker key he broke the stitching near the bulge his hand had found. When it was open enough he reached in and pulled out an undeveloped roll of film.

"Well, this answers a lot of questions." JB held the film out to Len. "Put this in your purse. And let's get out of here."

JB went to the phone by the door, picked it up, waited a moment, then said, "Yes. We're ready to leave now." A second later the door was opened by the assistant. "We were going to take the coat with us. However, there's a spot where the lining has come unstitched. Have it fixed, please."

Len dropped the coat into the man's arms. It piled up so that only the shine of his bald head showed above it. As JB took Len's elbow they heard a muffled, "Of course, right away."

Then they both left the shop. Len's feathers bouncing merrily.

When JB returned to the building he found that Toby was in the middle of preparing his promised dinner. As Toby handed over a drink to JB he said, "I saw Len when he got back. He said the drag thing went well, but he wouldn't give any details. You found something?"

"Actually we did. A roll of film. I put it in the shop to be developed on my way home..." JB then told Toby what had happened. "...so when Len let out that 'Crips' I thought the attendant was going to figure it out. But he didn't and let us in. Where is Len anyway?"

"He's upstairs. Getting out of costume. He should be here in a little while. He's coming to dinner. That's OK, isn't it?"

"Sure. It is your house." JB got up from the couch and crossed to the kitchen area. He put his arms around Toby and kissed the back of his neck. "And you can even cook. You can't be for real."

"What do you mean?"

"Well, several things. You're a nice guy. Great sex. You like Len. And you even cook. That's one hell of a combination."

"I can also knit, do household repairs, and get rid of yellow waxy buildup." He turned and leaned against the stove, crossed his arms and looked directly into JB's eyes. "What will it get me?"

JB's thoughts raced, crashed, and jumbled around in his head. This is going way to fast...God, he's cute....I've only known him for four days!... What's for dinner?...I know practically nothing about him....My Lord, he's cute...Is it hot in here?...But I do like the feelings when I'm around him...He's so cute....I've got to work on that chapter later...But he's so young...And cute....Do I have clean underwear for tomorrow?...I'm just too settled...So damn cute...*I've got the sun in the mornin' and the moon at night*...Oh great, now I'm doing Merman impressions...*I had a dream, a dream about you, Baby*.... Stop it!.. ..No more Ethel...Think about how cute he is....Where the hell is Len?...Could it actually work with Toby?

Toby was still looking at him and waiting for an answer to his question. JB opened his mouth not quite sure what would come out, and the front door buzzer sounded. "That's Len," JB stammered. He leaned forward and kissed Toby on the forehead. "I can't answer your question right now. But, believe me, it truly deserves an answer. Can we talk later?"

Disappointment shadowed Toby's face. "I guess," he said. JB hugged him and they held on for a few seconds. Then JB went to answer the door.

Len was standing in the doorway with a bottle of wine in his hand and a plastic rose in his teeth. He flung the flower over his shoulder and clutching his hands around the neck on the bottle of wine, he said, "Mama. Mama, I' m pretty."

"Natalie Wood as Louise in *Gypsy*. I was just thinking about her. Ethel singing *Everything's Coming Up Roses*, I mean. Good God, Len, how gay can the two of us get?"

"I just spent the last two hours in drag. How much more gay do I have to be?"

"True. That does make you pretty gay. You win. You're gayer than me."

JB shut the door. Len handed the wine to Toby and turned back to JB. Then he raised one arm straight above his head and threw the other arm out to his side. Holding the pose he said, "You have to admit I looked absolutely fabulous in that chinchilla. And, JB, we got away with it."

"Right," JB answered. "And that film we found may lead us to the killer. We done good, kiddo."

Len went to Toby's small bar and started mixing himself a drink. "Do you really think that film can lead to the murderer? It might have fallen through a hole in her pocket. It might just be pictures of Cousin Morrie's Bar Mitzvah. A Hadassa meeting. An orgy."

"We'll get the pictures back tomorrow. We can see what they are then. If they're snapshots of Sylvia's last daytrip to the Meadowlands, it's nothing. But if they're what I think they are it'll confirm what I'm pretty sure was going on."

"And what was that, Mr. Chan?" Len sat on the couch and put his feet on the coffee table.

"Number one son ask excellent question. Answer is, Mrs. Lucan had herself a nice little business going."

"What kind of business?"

"Blackmail."

"No shit!" Len sat up. Toby stopped setting the table.

"It's obvious when you look at it all together. After all she did have some prior experience with her ex-husband. And blackmailing others made it possible for her to stop extorting money from him. That was a year ago he told Kelly. She only had one more thing to sell him and she decided to keep that as insurance. So, she started being a freelance busybody here in this building. The notebook we found is her list of victims and the film is her evidence. What she had on each of the people. From what it looks like she was doing pretty well at it too. She bought most of the art in her apartment with blackmail money. That explains the large deposits and withdrawals in her bankbook."

"Then one of the people she blackmailed killed her."

"That's what I would guess," JB said. "The main problem now is we can't figure out the phrases she used in the notebook. That's where we're stuck. Trying to guess what twists and turns her devious little mind took to come up with that nonsense to disguise her victim's identities."

Toby put a large bowl of linguine with sauce on the table. "Dinner's ready, guys."

While they ate they talked of politics, the weather, the latest Broadway shows, but the conversation inevitably got back to Mrs. Lucan and her notebook.

When Toby heard the phrases she used he said, "It sounds more like descriptions than names. Or twists on names, maybe?"

"That could be," JB said. He then became silent while he examined the puzzle backwards, forwards, and upside down in his head. They finished eating and moved to the couch for coffee. JB followed but still was silent.

Toby looked at Len. He shrugged. "When he gets like this there's no getting through to him." Len picked up the TV listings and flipped through them. "Oh, look. Channel Nine has *Breakfast At Tiffany's* on tonight. I loved Audrey Hepburn in that.

"I liked her in *Roman Holiday* too," Toby said.

"Or *The Nun's Story*. All that suffering. And didn't she look fabulous in a habit. All in black with those white accents."

JB's head snapped up. "The Pope's Son!"

Len and Toby stared at him.

"Don't you remember? In *The Nun's Story*. When Audrey Hepburn was ordained a nun they put a wedding band on her hand. She was married to Christ. Who is Christ's representative on Earth for every Catholic?"

"The Pope," Toby said.

"Right. Then who would be the mother of a son by the Pope?"

"A nun! Did I guess right?" Len clapped his hands.

"Yes! That's just what I meant."

"Well, you've got something there, but what exactly?"

"I don't know. I'm perfectly aware this isn't the fourteenth century and nuns no longer mess with priests or Pope's. Damn."

"Is it getting dark in here?" Toby leaned over and switched on the tension lamp that sat next to JB. Its light struck JB directly in the face. That caused him to squint, so he reached out to adjust it. Then he hesitated. He let the light stay on his face as if soaking up the heat from it. A moment later he turned back. "Len, do you still have that *Whatever Happened To* book? The one that tells where old movie stars are now."

"Sure. It's upstairs. Do you want it?"

"That's why I asked."

Len went to get the book. He was back in a few minutes and handed it over to JB.

JB opened the book to the index, ran his finger down the list of names, and turned to the page with information on Hope Gordon.

"Do you remember her, Len? She made a big splash in the sixties. She starred in a couple of big pictures and got lots of publicity. The next Grace Kelly, or Kim Novak, or some such. Anyway, she married the director of her last picture and then, a few years later, went through a messy divorce and custody battle for her kid. It destroyed her career. Divorce was pretty scandalous back then. We weren't as tolerant in those days. She disappeared in the seventies, but I remembered something I'd read about her." He quickly skimmed the book. "Here it is." He read, "*She put her son in boarding school and gave up the glamour of Hollywood to become Sister Hope Evangeline, a cloistered nun at the Sister's of Charity convent in Magdelain, Ohio.*"

"Ohio?" Len looked at JB. "Why does that ring a bell?"

JB went on. "And who was the director Hope Gordon married and then divorced? None other than William Terillo."

"Terillo? You don't mean our Mr. Terillo over in apartment 1-A?"

"You bet I do. The porn star Johnny Huge is a son of a nun! And probably a blackmail victim."

JB sat back. On his face was a grin. There was one less puzzle to solve.

"Wait a second," Len said. "Are you telling me that you got all that from the mention of an old Audrey Hepburn movie?"

"Right. And thanks for mentioning it."

"Your welcome, but really, JB, how much more gay can you possibly be? With that trick you reclaim the title. You are the gayest. I mean, I'm not even that gay when I have sex."

JB knocked on the door of apartment 1-A. Toby and Len were behind him. The door opened and Johnny Terillo stood there in a pair of gym shorts. He was wiping his forehead with a towel. A set of chrome weights was spread out on the floor of the apartment. He looked at the three of them and then behind him. "What's the matter? Am I lifting too loud?"

"No, not at all." JB said. We're sorry to disturb you so late, but we're here to ask a few more questions. If that's OK?"

Johnny nodded and they all went inside the apartment. The three of them watched as Johnny went over and lay down on his weight bench. His hands went up and then closed around the bar over his head. He lifted and started to pump the heavy weight up and down above his chest.

"So, what is it?" The weight went up and he inhaled.

"You work out a great deal, don't you, Johnny?"

The weight came down and he exhaled. "Have to. Part of my job." He inhaled and the weight went back up.

"Just what is your job?"

Down. Exhale. "Films. And I get paid to date."

"You mean you're a gigolo?"

Up, Inhale. "I prefer escort."

Len said, "Escorting must pay pretty well. Those chrome weights of yours cost big bucks."

Down. Exhale. "I'm a very good escort."

The bar clanged back into its holder. Johnny sat up and looked over at them. "What's this all about anyway? What are these questions for?"

JB asked, "You say you do films?"

"Yeah," Johnny said slowly.

"Wouldn't be hard core, would they?"

He sighed. "So you figured it out, huh? Well, whatta' ya want? An autograph or a free show?"

Len perked up. "You do private shows too?"

Johnny jerked his thumb at Toby. "Ask him. He's watched a few matinee's since I moved in. I knew he was peeking over the fence watching me sunbathe. Get your rocks off, buddy?"

Toby's face turned crimson and he looked down at the floor.

Len jumped to Toby's defense. "Well, you can't blame him since you're the one who's been putting it on display. The only thing missing is a price tag hanging from the end like on Minnie Pearl's hat."

"Hell, you're no better than he is. The first time you were here all you did was look down. I could have had three eyes on my forehead and you wouldn't have known it."

"I was more interested in that other trio you own! So what? That is your stock in trade isn't it?"

"All right, both of you," JB interrupted. "This isn't getting us anywhere. May I ask another question?"

But Johnny wouldn't let it go. "Is that what you think I am? Just a piece of beef on the hoof?" He stood up. "All right. If that's all I am, then take a look at this, mister!" He grabbed the waistband of his shorts and pushed down.

His balls hung low and heavy in their sac. His cock stood away from his body surrounded by the dark patch of his pubic hair. The veins running along his member filled until he had a full ten-and-a-half inch erection. He reached down and wrapped his hand around it. "Grade A prime, boys. Just another piece of meat."

Len stared at the huge cock. Toby's head stayed focused on the floor. If it was possible he was more chagrined by this turn of events. JB continued to look straight into Johnny's face.

Just as Len was about come back with some sort of remark JB took hold of his arm. "Shut up, Len. Don't make this worse. All of us are already suitably embarrassed. Johnny, I'm sorry if you think we were criticizing you for the way you make a living. That's not our intention."

Johnny got a towel from the bench and wrapped it around his waist. It tented at the front from his now partial erection. "And I don't mean to be so damn defensive. I hate these frigging videos I do. But they pay well. I have to pay for school. I'm at Visual Arts."

"I know porn is considered sleazy and disreputable by some people..."

"That's not it," Johnny said as he sat down on the bench. "I could care less what the bluenoses think. It's the films themselves. Crummy scripts. When there's any story at all. Lousy lighting. Tacky sets. Horrendous acting. And the camera work. I could do better with an Instamatic."

Toby had a look of surprise. "You sound like you want to direct. Isn't that a bit of a cliche?"

"Cliche or not its what I want to do. Then I can get out and leave the porn business to the incompetents that run it now. But that's someday. Listen, I'm really sorry. You said you have another question?"

"Yeah. I wanted to ask you about the trip you took to Ohio. To visit your Mother. At the convent."

Johnny at first just stared at the three men, then it seemed as if any self-confidence he may have still possessed drained away. The rest of his erection went limp. He covered his face with his hands. Moments later, when he looked up, there were tears running down his cheeks. He seemed a vulnerable and frightened child. In a voice that was soft and barely audible he said, "How did you find out?"

"From Mrs. Lucan," JB said. "We found her

notebook."

Johnny shook his head. "I should have known she would keep notes."

"She was blackmailing you, wasn't she? She had threatened to expose your porn movies to your Mother. The confessions, as she called them, were actually payments, right?"

Johnny nodded. "It would probably kill my Mother if she found out how I make my living. She thinks I'm in advertising."

Len said, "You are to some extent. I mean you are publicizing a product. If you think of yourself as your own product that is?" Len took his rationalization farther. "You haven't really lied at all, Johnny, since what you do is really just another form of advertising, right?"

"I couldn't let that evil woman send any of those films to Mother. So I paid the old viper to keep quiet. You see why I had to do it, right?"

"Of course, Johnny. I suppose I can understand," JB said. "But what about the night Mrs. Lucan was killed?"

"I told you before. I was in Ohio. I didn't come back until Sunday evening. What are you getting at?"

"Someone who is being blackmailed could think he has a good reason to kill, Johnny."

"What!" His voice had regained its strength. "Wait a minute. Sure, I paid her. And I hated her for it. But I didn't kill her. I can't say I'm sorry that she's dead, but I didn't do it. Just a second."

He jumped from the bench and went over to a table. He picked up an envelope and threw it toward JB. "That's my proof. I wasn't even in the city when it happened."

The envelope contained a used airline ticket from Ohio to New York, leaving Ohio the previous Sunday afternoon. JB looked up and handed the ticket back.

Then he reached into his pocket and took out Mrs. Lucan's notebook. He tore out the pages Johnny's information was written on and handed them over to him.

"I would keep the airline tickets in case the police question you. The pages you can destroy. You don't have to pay anymore blackmail, Johnny. You're free."

Johnny held on to the pages and said, "Thank you." Then he started to tear the papers into small, and then smaller, pieces.

B ack in Toby's apartment JB flopped down on the couch and put his arms behind his head. "I guess that proves I was right in what I suspected about Mrs. Lucan."

Len sat on JB's left, his face chiseled by the light. His eyes had a dark film floating on the rounded surface.

JB went on. "What we have to do now is figure out who the rest of the victims are and confront them. One of them is a murderer."

Len rolled his head back and forth slowly and

sighed. "Can we do it later, JB. I don't feel much like playing detective right now." He leaned forward and clasped his hands together. "In my head I keep replaying Johnny's face when we told him what we knew. He was shattered. We broke him, JB. We opened up his head and wrenched out something private and secret."

"No, Len, you and I didn't. Mrs. Lucan did. She was the one who stole the secret from him. She was the one who twisted it and made it seem perverse and ugly. For money. What we did was give it back to him. He can stuff it away again or leave it in the open. He has to decide."

"Then we did a good thing?" Len replied. "Then why don't I feel like I'm wearing shiny armor?"

"Because we just looked into the face of something hideous. When a secret is exposed it has form and shape, like a malignant tumor surgically removed and thrown into the middle of a room. If you've kept it hidden for a long time it's large and putrid, and it pulsates like some science fiction monster. That's what secret's are. Monsters that live inside you. They grow and ruin your life. You have to spend every waking moment trying to keep them hidden. You can't trust anyone. What if they find out? You can't build a relationship—not when the foundation it's built on is a lie. You can't sleep at night because you're afraid someone might have found you out. Someone like Mrs. Lucan."

"What a truly despicable woman she was."

"Yeah, maybe she was. She certainly wallowed in a dirty little swamp. And maybe she deserved what she got. I don't know. What I do know is you don't deserve to be blamed for her death. Remember that Kelly still has you as his number one suspect. That means we have to find out who killed her. So, let's get to it."

Len shook his head. "Tomorrow. OK? Right now

I think I just want to go to bed." Len stood up. When JB reached forward and took his hand Len bent down and gave him a hug. Len said, "Good night." Then he left.

"He really has a great deal of compassion," JB said to Toby. "There's just a whole lot of cynicism covering it up."

JB realized that Toby hadn't uttered a word since they all entered the apartment a whole conversation ago. He turned to him. "Are you all right?"

Toby nodded, but his face said the opposite. JB held his arms out. Toby moved over and snuggled in closely against JB's chest.

"I feel bad for Johnny too."

"So do I, Toby. But Johnny will be all right. In fact, he'll probably be better now. He doesn't have to hide anymore. How freeing that must feel. To know you don't have to lie anymore."

"I know." Toby's voice was soft and pensive.

JB wondered what was wrong with him? There's more to this than just embarrassment at being caught spying on a hunk over a backyard fence. But what? I suppose there's nothing terrific about trying to solve any murder. Especially one that's turning out to be as sordid as this one is. That must be it. It even turns my stomach to see the negative side of decent people exposed. It's like finding out that Mother Teresa played the horses in her spare time. It must upset him too.

"I'm glad Johnny didn't do it," Toby said in the same small voice as before.

"He was lucky he still had the ticket. Most people throw them away after a long flight."

"Not that long. It almost takes longer to get out to the airport."

"Really? How long is it to Ohio?"

"About two hours is all."

JB didn't say anything. Toby sat up. "JB?"

"What? Oh, I was just thinking. It's possible that Johnny could have got here and back in time to make that flight from Ohio again."

"But why make two flights?"

"If you have murder in mind it's your alibi. But that doesn't make sense. It's way too complicated. Isn't it?"

Neither of them said anything. They sat together on the couch, each in their own heads. Toby didn't bring up their pre-dinner conversation again. JB was just as glad since he hadn't yet formed an answer to Toby's question. After awhile they got up and went to the bedroom. Each of them had a night of restless sleep ahead of them.

Around midnight JB was awakened by Toby's thrashing in the midst of a bad dream. JB reached over and laid his hand on Toby's back. Toby quieted down and grabbed JB's hand. They stayed in that position for the rest of the night.

The next morning Toby was still in his non-talkative mood from the night before. JB, not at all sure what to do, decided not to try to cajole him and ended up leaving him to his quietude. JB sat at the kitchen table and studied Mrs. Lucan's notebook.

Her mind was too convoluted, too devious, and to nuts for JB to figure out which name fit which person in the building. Other than making a guess that the question marks belong to the rude guy nobody knew in 4-B, there was no real proof that she had only been hitting on this building's tenants. In a city of over eight million people it could be anyone. He decided this would have to wait until he had the pictures. Which he'd get as soon as the store opened.

JB put the notebook aside and took a sip of the coffee Toby had made for him. "This coffee is great," he said. Anything to get Toby talking, even if it did sound like a silly TV commercial. "What is it?"

"It's a French blend I get at this shop over on East 65th. I'll..."

There was a crashing sound from somewhere close in the building.

"What the hell?" Toby started for the front door. As he did there was another crash of something large being hit, then toppling and breaking on the floor.

"It sounds like someone's having a fight."

"It is," Toby said. "It's those two in 1-B." As the sounds of violence grew Toby went for his keys. He ran down the hall, with JB close behind him, and then pounded on the door.

"Open up in there! This is the Super!"

In reply Toby heard the sound of a chair being smashed on a table. Toby found the right key and threw open the door.

He was greeted by total m a y h e m. A bookcase had been overturned and its contents were spilled all over the room. Shards of broken china glittered in the light from the window, which now had a crack running from the top to the bottom sill. Broken pieces of furniture were scattered all over. In the center of this mess were the two boys. Boy #1 had the bunched up shirtfront of Boy #2 in his left hand. His right hand was raised over his head holding a chair leg poised to bash Boy #2's head in.

Toby shouted, "Hey!"

Boy #1 turned his head and looked at them. "Get out of here, faggots!" he shouted.

Boy #2 saw his attackers newly directed attention as a chance to get away and grabbed at it. He pushed himself backward over the back of the couch they were standing behind. As he fell he pulled Boy #1 off balance and both ended up in a tangle of arms and legs on the couch's cushions. Boy #1's legs stuck straight up, his feet doing a dance on thin air.

The silver tips on his shoes glittered from the light streaming in the window, just as the glaze glinted on the broken pottery scattered around the room.

"Wait just a minute," JB said. He moved across the room to where the fighters were. He reached and grabbed the back of Boy #1's coat. Then he lifted him up off the couch.

JB started walking backward with him toward the door. Once there he turned and pushed the boy, smashing him against the wall, which caused a picture still hanging to bounce from the force. The boy raised both his arms to protect himself.

"You want a fight, you little bastard?" JB flicked the boy's hands aside, took hold of his coat lapels and lifted him. The boy's toes just barely touched the floor. "I'll fight you. I'll beat your head in until you have to fart to clear your throat!" He lowered the boy while he kept one coat lapel gripped in his hand. JB's other hand drew back and formed a fist.

A second before he was about to let go his punch Toby grabbed his arm. "JB, what in hell are you doing?" JB turned his head. Toby could see that his eyes were muddy with anger. He couldn't believe the rage he saw in this up to now calm and peaceful man. "You'll kill him. For God's sake, let him go!"

They all stood frozen in this tableau for several seconds. Toby was holding JB's arm. JB was holding the boy's coat. The boy was holding his hands up to cover his face. Then JB seemed to return to his normal self. The boy lowered his hands and said, "What's the matter, Nancy? Afraid you'll break a nail?"

JB looked at Toby. Toby shrugged. JB opened his fist and swung giving the boy an open handed slap that knocked his head backward against the wall. The picture bounced again and tilted on its wire. It made a loud scraping noise as it slid upside down.

JB pulled the now goggle-eyed boy from the wall and threw him onto the couch next to Boy #2. He stood over them, his breathing hard and rapid.

"These bastards broke into Len's apartment. They're the ones who beat both of us when we caught them in the middle of it."

Toby said, "How do you know that?"

"When they were fighting here on the couch the light from the window flashed off this weasel's shoe tips. I remembered seeing the same flash just before I passed out. When I saw it here it clicked."

Boy #1 had regained some of his senses and turned to Toby. "This pansy's crazy. I never did any such thing."

Boy #2 shouted, "Yes he did! He did it!"

Boy #1 yelled, "You rotten little thief!" He jumped across the couch at the other boy. Boy #2 rolled into a ball and screeched, "Help! He'll kill me."

Toby grabbed one of them, JB the other, and they pulled them apart. "You touch each other again and you'll both be dead," Toby threatened. They calmed down enough to sit glaring at each other.

JB flicked a speck of imaginary lint off Boy #2's shoulder. "As a matter of fact, you both did the break in and the attack. And you, my little cellar rat, are going to explain why, or I'll let your friend here have at you,"

The boy had to decide if he was better off with JB and Toby, or the homicidal maniac who sat across from him. "It was the old woman. The one who died," he explained. "She was the reason. She tried to shake us down. To blackmail us. She was going to turn us into the fuzz. When we found out she died we knew she couldn't anymore, but there was still the evidence she had. We had to get that. We did her place first. Then we figured that since you and your friend have been asking questions about her you two had found it. So we did your friends place. We had just about finished when he came in. We hid behind the door and conked him. Then we heard you coming."

"So you conked me too. But you didn't get the evidence, right?"

"No. But when you didn't try to blackmail us we figured we were safe. We opened up shop again."

"What kind of shop?"

"They're drug dealers, Toby. They have a regular hallucinogenic supermarket here."

"Drugs!"

"Right, you damn queer," Boy #1 said. "We've been dealing out of here since we moved in. Right under your nose. Until that old bag screwed it up. Then when you fairies started asking questions we figured we had to do something to protect ourselves."

JB talked directly to Boy #1. "You know, Toby stopped me from beating the crap out of you when I realized you were the one who decked me, but if you keep up this homophobic stuff I'm hearing from your mouth nothing will stop me. I'll wrap your asshole around your wrist like a bracelet."

"Fuck you, faggot."

JB brought his hands up to his head and began to sway back and forth. With a mock moan he said, "Oh, no! My God! Please! I've never heard such terrible words! No one in my entire existence has ever called me that before! I'm devastated! I'm desolate! I'm wounded to the very soul of my being! I can't stand it! Oh, the humanity! I'll just have to kill myself."

JB reached down and dragged the boy from the couch up to within a few inches of his face. "Now keep your garbage mouth shut!"

He dropped him back down and turned to Boy #2. "Now do you want to give me any trouble?" The boy shook his head. "Then what was the evidence Mrs. Lucan had on you two?"

"She told us she had pictures of us with a delivery. She took them through the window there. We knew she wasn't bluffing because she knew all the details. She had to have actually seen it. We had to get the pictures. They showed us with over two grand worth of coke."

"So, first you killed her and then went back for the pictures?"

"No! We didn't kill her. We told the truth the day you were here. We were at the Click until six. You can check. Call the club. They'll tell you."

"You can bet we will. What's your name anyway?"

"Kenny. Kenny Plutt."

It figures, JB thought. Ugly business, ugly name.

Toby asked, "Why were you two fighting?"

Boy #1 looked at Kenny. "That bastard is using. Way more than his share. He's been cutting the profits. I'll kill him!"

"No. I don't think so," Toby said. "What you are going to do is get out of this building by this afternoon. Forget the lease. You broke that already. And my boss will back me up. You don't like blackmail? Well listen to this. You get out today or you both are in jail tomorrow. Do you understand." The boys nodded. "Good! Let's get out of here, JB. They have some packing to do. Besides the stench from these scuzballs is making me sick."

JB put his hand on Kenny's shoulder. "Listen. You' have about forty seconds to get your stuff and get out of here. So your buddy here won't hurt you."

Kenny jumped up from the couch and ran to the bedroom. In seconds he was back with a length of rope and a baseball bat. He pushed Boy #1 forward, pulled his arms back, and wrapped the rope around his wrists several times, then went to his ankles. After knotting the rope he stood up.

"That'll hold him until he calms down." He held up the bat. "And this will make sure he stays real calm."

"You mean to tell me that after all that he's done to you you're still going to stay?"

"Sure. Where would I go? I love him."

In unison JB and Toby said, "You what!"

"All that homophobia is just a cover. He's afraid someone might actually think he's queer. But he's way more interested than he let's on. He's been teasing me for months now. And finally, I've got him right where I want him."

JB shook his head. "You are one sick puppy. You should also make sure those ropes are good and tight."

"I will. But I don't think he'll argue too much."

He went over to his captive, bent over him, and put a hand on his thigh.

"What the hell?"

Kenny leaned into him and kissed him on the mouth. Boy #1 sputtered and started to say something when Kenny put his hand over the boy's mouth.

"You are about to learn something new about yourself, baby."

Kenny's other hand started to undo Boy #1's shirt buttons.

As JB and Toby left, JB turned back and looked. Boy #1's eyes were closed and a small smile was playing on his lips.

"Hey!" The boy opened his eyes and looked over at JB. "What's your name, weasel? Just in case I ever have a pet cockroach I want to name."

The boy gasped as Kenny's tongue made a circle around his navel. "Blondel. Blondel Druck." He moaned as the tongue found its target.

JB nodded. "I should have known," he said.

Toby opened the door to his apartment. "JB, please explain what in blue blazes that boy could possibly see in that jerk?" He sat at the kitchen table and waited for an answer.

JB followed Toby in and sat across from him. "Beyond the fact that there's no accounting for taste? Even really poor taste. I suppose it could be the old Don Quixote syndrome."

"Huh?"

"The challenge is the turn on. The impossible dream and all that crap. Some queers think the epitome of a real man is someone straight. And I use that term loosely. God knows why that is considered desirable? Straight men are usually boring as hell in bed, and their conversation always seems to center on sports and farting. So, go figure?"

JB got up and went to the phone, picked it up and dialed information. He got his number then re-dialed. When the call was answered he talked for about five minutes. "Well, thank you. You've been a great help," he finished.

Toby, meanwhile, sat at the table stewing. "You know what really pisses me off," he said. "It's those two selling drugs out of this building. How could I have missed it?"

JB hung up the phone. "You probably didn't miss anything, Toby. They couldn't have sold much out of this place, if any. They didn't have the time and probably not the stock to sell from here too." Toby gave him a look that asked for an explanation. JB went on. "Back when disco was still going strong most of the clubs had some guy selling drugs to the dancers. Hell, in San Francisco a couple of the places on Polk Street even had a queen walking around with a tray hanging off his shoulders, like cigarette girls in a Forties nightclub. But he went around calling out 'Poppers....Acid....Ludes'. Kenny and Blondel seem to be the current version." JB jerked his thumb at the phone. "I spoke with the manager of the Click. He knows both of the guys and will swear that they were at a party the night Mrs. Lucan was killed."

"Then they couldn't have done it. But they should still be in jail."

"Then why don't you turn them in? The phone is right over there."

"I can't, JB. This building has had too much happen here this week, what with bodies in bathtubs, and break-in's. My da....Uh, the owner would have a cow if I brought down a drug bust too. There's no way

I'd keep this job. No. The best thing is to just get the scumbags out of here."

"I guess so, but I wouldn't be so sure that this buildings problems are over yet. There's still a killer to find." JB picked up the notebook from the table. "Well, we can cross 'Winters Vogues' off the list."

"Is that who she meant? Those two?"

JB nodded.

"How did you know?" Toby asked.

"I used crazy logic. It looks like Mrs. Lucan had a Gracie Allen fixation. You know how Gracie always started from a mistaken assumption, but each step thereafter was logical and made sense. Well, that kinda gave it to me. It goes like this." JB held up a finger. "When it's winter you get snow. Logical?" He held up another finger. "Snow is a classic slang term for cocaine. Still logical?" JB held up a third finger. "Those two boys dress in the latest style so they are in vogue." He closed the three fingers together. "Ta-da. Winter's Vogue."

"I'm impressed. You figured that out from just knowing they sold drugs?"

"Well, that and her notes." JB handed the notebook over to Toby. He read—*Used film through window and got the goods. They are lulus.*

"You fake!" He laughed.

JB laughed too. "You should do that more often, Toby. It's nice to hear. Listen, I have to go get the pictures from the photo shop. Will I see you later?"

"Uh...Yeah. Sure. Even better, JB, why don't you call. We can set something up."

"Well, OK?"

"JB, I'm sorry about this lousy mood I'm in. It's just everything that's going on. I'll get over it. Soon. You go on."

"Sure. I'll call you later."

As JB took the short walk to the photo shop he pondered Toby's mood and how Toby had left their seeing each other again up in the air. Why the hesitancy to make a date? Have I done something wrong? Everything seemed fine before. Now he seems distant. I suppose it could be just a mood. But, damnt, it doesn't matter anymore if we've only known each other for a few days. I like him. And I really would like to keep on seeing him. But that's really up to him, isn't it? If he doesn't want to see me I can't force him.

At the camera shop the clerk handed over the envelope of pictures, then, as he looked down his nose, said "You know, sir, we're not supposed to develop these sorts of pictures. Bare breasts and assorted other—ahem—illegal acts. By law I'm supposed to report all such photos."

JB reached into his pocket. "And how much extra did you say that would be?" That's my New York, he thought. You can find anything and everything you want...from salacious photos to dwarfs riding donkeys in lace panties. Either the donkey or the dwarf...as long as you look hard enough and have enough money.

JB forked over an extra ten that he was sure would never show up in the cash drawer. The clerk smiled a slimy smile and JB left the shop. He headed for Len's apartment building.

When he turned the corner from Third Avenue he saw there was a commotion up ahead. A large group of people was crowded around five cars pulled up in front of Len's building. Three of them were marked police car with their red and blue lights flashing like twinkling Christmas bulbs.

There were a couple of uniformed police standing about controlling the small crowd. Another group of three men stood inside a cordoned off area.

JB worked his way through the crowd to the front and saw that Lieutenant Kelly was one of the trio. He waved and called his name. Kelly nodded at him, then returned his attention to the other men. A minute later the men left Kelly, walked over to the lobby door and went inside.

Kelly turned again, nodded to the guard and JB was let pass. JB walked up to the Lieutenant and asked, "What's going on?"

"We caught ourselves a murderer, Bent." Kelly actually had a slight smile on his face. It looked almost painful.

"My God, Kelly, not Len? I told you he couldn't have..."

"Hold on, Bent. It's not your friend. Yet. This one is an escaped killer from upstate. Willie Hackshaw. We located him last night. I heard he was in this building and came along for the ride."

"You mean he's hiding out here?" Kelly said yes. "It must be that guy up in 4-B. The one who moved in last week."

"That's the one. Although how the Super didn't know who he was I can't guess. His picture was everywhere."

"His face is all bandaged so you can't see it. And Toby said the apartment was rented by an agent. So he never saw the guy at all. Neither has anyone else from what I can tell."

"Except, apparently, you. I thought I told you to keep your nose out of our cases, Bent." The smile had disappeared from Kelly's face.

"Well, we've all talked about it. That's all right, isn't it?"

"I guess. As long as that's all."

JB didn't have to answer. At that moment the two plainclothes officers who had previously gone into the building come out the front door. Between them they held the bandaged fugitive, Willie Hackshaw, by each of his arms. His hands were handcuffed behind him. The crowd around the building seemed to make a collective step forward at his appearance. When he saw the crowd surge toward him he pulled back from his captors. A struggle started between them as the cops tried to aim Willie toward a waiting car, and he tried to get away from the people jostling him. In the rumpus JB spotted an object fall from Willie's coat pocket.

Flashbulbs started popping from reporter's cameras in the crowd. That spooked Willie even more and he tried to break from the detectives at his side. And for a second he actually did. There was a gasp from the crowd. The police grabbed Willie again and then forcibly led him toward the open door of the car. They pushed his head down and shoved him inside, tumbled in back with him and shut the door. The car took off with its siren blasting. The reporters rushed after it snapping pictures as they went. The crowd dispersed leaving Kelly and JB standing alone in front of the building.

"Why the bandages, Kelly?"

"I'm not sure. Maybe he had some plastic surgery to fix his looks. Crooks always think that's going to work."

"And maybe Mrs. Lucan actually found out who he was and he killed her. Did you think of that?"

"You never stop do you? When we get Willie to the station we'll ask that. Among other questions."

"I just want to make sure you follow up on every lead, Kelly. That's all."

JB took a step back and started moving his foot around searching for the object he had seen drop from Hackshaw's pocket earlier. From a distance he looked as if he was doing ballet exercises. Second position, fourth position, then fifth position.

"Bent, the police aren't idiots you know? We

have enough sense to follow up on the obvious. What the hell are you doing?"

"Just looking for something I dropped. Here it is." He bent and picked up the object. It was a pack of matches from the Cie Bella Italian restaurant down in Little Italy. JB recognized the name as a notorious organized crime hangout. What was it with mobsters and food? And what was Willie Hackshaw doing in Little Italy? JB didn't have a clue. He heard Kelly talking at him so he stood back up.

"What was that, Kelly? My mind was miles away."

"I was asking if you wanted to come to the station and see for yourself that we asked Hackshaw about the Lucan matter. Witnessing what we police do might improve your opinion of us. Your books have us missing evidence right and left. Trust me, we don't miss much."

"That was literary license, Kelly." JB put Willie Hackshaw's matchbook into his pocket and walked over to Kelly's car.

Looking through the one way window into the interrogation room at Bellevue's prisoner ward JB felt like he was watching a colorized version of a Thirties horror movie.

Willie was sitting, still swathed in bandages, at a table in the center of the room. A single lamp with an industrial shade hung above his head. One Uniform, one Plainclothes, and a Doctor were crowded around him firing questions. It's was a scene right out of the old Universal horror pictures. *Big House Mummy.*

In front of him, instead of a cauldron of boiling tana leaves, Willie had a bowl filled to overflowing with cigarette butts. Not life-giving by any means. Even Willie's gauze wrapped fingers had yellowed from the nicotine in his chain-smoked cigarettes.

"All right, Willie," the Plainclothes said. "What's with the bandage's?"

"None uh yer friggin' bizness, copper." Willie even sounded like a character from an old gangster movie.

"Let's just find out, huh, Willie." The Uniform reached over and grabbed Willie's left wrist. He pulled it across the table and held it flat. "Doc?"

Holding a pair of surgical scissors, the Doctor cut the bandages from the back of Willie's hand. When they were removed the hand looked pale and wrinkled as if it had been in water too long.

The Uniform flipped the hand over like a dead fish and said, "So, you had the fingerprints removed. That's too bad, Willie. It means we'll have to re-print you. I don't think the ink will help your hand heal very well. It might even cause an infection. Did you know a person could die from an infection, Willie?"

Willie took a drag off his cigarette and blew smoke into the Uniform's face. "Did ya know ya could die from secondhand smoke, copper?"

The Plainclothes sat at the table. "Willie this is getting us nowhere. Just answer our questions and we'll leave you alone. OK? There are four questions, Willie, and they're easy. Who helped you escape? Who was the surgeon? Who got you the apartment you were hiding in? Did you kill Sylvia Lucan?"

JB sat forward to hear better. Willie leaned back and asked, "Who?"

"Come on, Willie. The lady that was killed in that same building on Sunday."

"Oh her. Nah. I din't ice her. All I know about that is these two fruits come aroun' askin' 'bout her. Ya know, ya cops should do somthin' 'bout all the queers in this town."

"We do, Willie. We let them have a parade every June."

"Dat's not what I mint."

"Let's cut the BS, Willie. You killed the old lady, didn't you? She found out who you were so you killed her."

"Christ, do ya tink' I'm stupid? Why da hell would I hav' stayed there if I offed de old broad?"

"Get the fingerprint kit for me, would you, Doc?"

"All right. I saw her once. But dats all. She came snoopin' 'roun my room on Saturday. I pulled my gun on her and she ran quick like. I din't see her afta' that."

"OK, Willie. That will have to do. For now. Let's move on to the next question. Who was the surgeon?"

"I won't tell ya nutin' more. I want my lawyer."

"Doc, lets see what's under this mask he's got. That'll at least tell us if the surgeon was any good."

The Doctor again stepped up and began to cut the gauze at the back of Willie's head.

Kelly, who was sitting next to JB in the listening room, spoke up. "Are you satisfied, Bent? We asked him about Mrs. Lucan, and he answered. His answer makes sense. He would have left that building pretty quick if he had killed the woman. He couldn't afford to draw any attention to himself. You can go now."

"Are you kidding? And miss the unveiling. I want to see if he looks like Frankenstein's monster or Marlene Dietrich."

"Find out from the papers like everyone else, Bent."

"Kelly, you have absolutely no sense of drama." JB went to the door and opened it. As he stepped through the doorway he heard the Uniform, in an awed voice, say, "Holy Cow, what did you do to yourself, Willie?"

Kelly pushed the door shut. JB shouted, "And you're timing stinks too!"

On the ride home from the hospital JB decided he wouldn't go see Toby when he got to the apartment. Considering all that had happened he would certainly have to be busy. Explaining the morning to his "da" and such.

JB settled back in the front seat of the squad car and tuned out the chatter of the policeman that Kelly had commandeered to drive him home.

Not seeing Toby also means I don't have to answer that question from last night. JB shook his head. I usually go roaring right in the middle of these kinds of situations—it's the Aries in me—but not this time. No way. I'm not completely sure why either. Other than the fact that the whole affair is moving to damn fast. There's something about Toby, some piece of the puzzle I can't find. Some key that won't fit the lock. Some....Good Lord, JB, cut the BS and admit it, you're scared. As hard as the breakup with Len was there is a degree of comfort in the current situation. You've got your work, a couple of nice guys to date and no one to answer to...except your editor. It's safe, secure, easy, and...and, damn it, kinda lonely. But do I want to give it up? For what? A twenty-five year old you can't figure out?

"Here we are, Mr. Bent."

"Where? Oh. Thanks for the ride, officer." JB climbed out of the car and watched it pull away. Then he turned, went into the building and straight up to Len's apartment.

When he opened the door Len was wearing a robe and had his face covered in shaving cream. In his hand was a tumbler half full of what could be water. JB was pretty sure it wasn't.

"You're starting early?" JB indicated the glass.

"Just a heart starter, old buddy." Len went back to the bathroom to finish shaving. He shouted, "Take a look at that book, JB. The one on the table. I did a bit of detective work of my own."

JB went over to the table and found the book Len indicated. It was a pictorial essay of the old Minsky's burlesque house called *Those Were The Days*. He picked it up, went to the bathroom doorway and asked, "What did you find in this?"

"I remembered one of Mrs. Lucan's phrases was 'Minsky's Cutie', so I thumbed through that to find a clue. And did I find one. Turn to page 169."

JB turned to the page. What he found was a picture of a dark-haired stripper with a great big grin meant just for the camera. She had her legs spread wide and was bent over at the waist showing Grand Canyon deep cleavage. She wore black mesh hose, high heels, a G-string, and a tasseled bra. Your regulation stripper uniform.

The caption under the picture read *STORMY DAZE: This beauty was one of the first of her generation to get her tassels to twirl in different directions on the 1960's burlesque circuit. This talent kept her stripping for many years. She was also said to be one of the most creative cussers in the entire business. Marriage finally took her away from the boards and she hasn't been heard of since.*

"OK," JB said. "So what? It's a picture of a stripper."

Len was moussing his hair. "Don't you see it? Add about three hundred and eighty pounds to good old Stormy and see if she doesn't seem familiar."

JB looked back at the picture, did the mental adjustment, and burst into laughter. "My God, this is too unbelievable! Stormy Daze is Mrs. Forsyth-Peal! Wait until that pretentious old harridan gets a load of this."

Len slid behind JB to the main room and started getting dressed. "No, JB. We can't just show it to her. We have to be more sneaky about it. It'll be much more fun."

JB sat at the table. "OK. I'll let you puncture her hypocritical balloons. But hers is another name we can match to the list."

Len slipped into his pants. "How many is that now?"

"Four."

"Really? I thought only two. Who are the others?"

"The rude guy upstairs was the question marks.

And the two boys in 1-B were 'Winters Vogue's'. They also have an alibi for the night."

"How did you figure they were that winter thing?"

"Because they're snow, or coke, sniffers... winter...and addicted to being fabulous... Vogue. Get it?" Len nodded. "And it got them thrown out of the building this morning."

"So the Frick and Frack of Ferragamo's are on the street. Good riddance, I say. Was that what all the noise was this morning?"

"How late did you wake up, Sleeping Beauty?"

"About eleven. And there wasn't any prince with a kiss either. Just a lot of noise."

"What you heard you indolent dolt was the sound of the police arresting Willie Hackshaw, the escaped murderer. He was caught upstairs in this building. in 4-B."

"What?"

"Yup, the rude guy upstairs is a convicted killer with a B-movie complex. Mrs. Lucan was lucky she didn't find out who he was or she might have died several hours earlier. And that took care of the questions marks on the list. So we still have five possibilities." JB held up the envelope of pictures. "But these might bring us closer to number one."

Len looked up from the buttons on his shirt. "Hey, you got the pictures. Don't just sit there. Open them up." He came over to the table as JB tore open the flap and pulled the eight-by-ten prints out of the envelope. He laid them on the table and spread them out. Len and JB leaned in closer.

There were several shots of Johnny Huge sunbathing, which Len slid over in front of himself. "I'll take care of these," he said.

"No you won't," JB said. "They're evidence. They'll go to the police eventually." He reached over and pulled them back.

While JB went to the next set of photos, Len surreptitiously reached over and managed to slip one of Johnny's pictures onto his lap without JB seeing him. Then he looked at JB and said, "What's next?"

JB held up a couple of shots of Boy #1 and his partner surrounded by stacks of baggies. The baggies were all filled with a suspicious looking white substance. Another photo caught one of the boys actually snorting some of the illicit product.

"That would have sent those two boys to jail all right," JB said.

"And those others would have destroyed Johnny. What else is there?"

JB held up a picture taken from the sidewalk in front of the building. It was of a man standing at the lobby door and looked as if it was taken during the colder months since the man had on a heavy overcoat. But no hat. The lobby door was open and someone was standing inside in conversation with the man outside. The interior shadowed the figure so you couldn't tell who it was. The man outside looked to be in his fifties with salt and pepper hair and a prominent nose.

Len looked at JB. "Who's that?"

"That is none other than Vincent 'The Iceman' Gallentini. He's a known Mafia don. And he's called 'Iceman' because that's what's supposed to run through his veins."

"Isn't that special. What's he doing at our building? Do you think he might have been the two boy's silent partner? Isn't the Mafia heavy into drugs?"

"That could be. But why would Mrs. Lucan want to take on the Mafia by blackmailing those boys. I can't believe she could she have been that stupid?"

"Maybe she was. And she got killed for her stupidity."

"Well, it could have been a Mafia hit. But it didn't look like one. It was too messy. And that would give us another possible killer. That's six. That's too many. I just don't think that was it. Her killing isn't the sort of thing the Mafia goes in for. Anyway, I I think it was something else." JB reached into his pocket and put the pack of matches on the table. "These fell out of Willie Hackshaw's pocket this morning."

"They're just a pack of matches."

"From a restaurant known to be where the mob hangs out. And now this picture. That's too much of a coincidence, Len."

"You mean this 'Iceman" guy has some connection with Willie Hackshaw?" JB nodded. "It's too far-fetched. Just because an escaped killer has some matches from where the Mafia eats doesn't mean he's one of them. Maybe he just likes Italian food."

"All right, maybe." JB picked up another picture. Taken from the doorway of Mrs. Lucan's apartment it was of Jennifer standing with a well-dressed man. They were wrapped around each other kissing. The man had brown hair and was clean-shaven. He had one arm around Jennifer; his other was inside her unbuttoned blouse cupping her exposed breast.

"Who is this? The face is covered." JB handed the picture to Len.

"But her tit's aren't," Len said while waggling his eyebrows in imitation of Groucho Marx.

JB searched the other pictures. He picked up another, looked at it, and then handed it to Len. This photo was taken a few moments later than the previous one. The man still held Jenny's breast but they had stopped kissing. He looked into her face with a much-photographed smile.

"I'll be damned."

"Hey, I've seen that guy before," Len said. "In the papers. That's Andrew Whitlow."

"You're right. He's the head of the Mayor's Transportation Task Force, isn't he?"

"That's the guy. So that's the rich sugar person Jenny's been seeing."

"And he's perfect to blackmail. He's married, and what...the father of two? Big in the city government. He's always in the papers at some function or another. There's talk he could be the next mayor, or so I've heard."

"I heard that too," Len said. "But he wouldn't take a chance on fouling that up by killing somebody, would he?"

"He would if he thought he could get away with it. Or Jennifer might have done it to protect him. I guess that makes her 'Bombay Season'."

"Really? How do you figure?"

"Stick with me on this. The old lady went pretty far to get this one. There are four seasons. Summer, winter, fall, and spring. Right?" Len nodded.

JB pointed at Len's glass of liquid. "What's in that glass? I'm not accusing, Len, I'm asking. OK?"

Len took hold of it and pulled it close just in case. "Gin. Why?"

"What's gin made from?"

Len thought a moment. "Juniper berries, right? Ain't nature grand?"

"So, that's it."

He gave JB a doubtful look. "Don't you get it? Gin and Jenny. Juniper and Jennifer."

"Oh. OK. Then what's Bombay?"

"You're the drinker here. You should know one of the top selling gins on the market."

"Of course," Len smiled. "Bombay. And the season would be spring. Jennifer Spring. Monsieur Perriot, you amaze me."

"Merci. And you, mon friend, are full of bullmerde. Len, we're going to have to talk to Jennifer. But before we do I'll need you to put the picture of Johnny you took back with the rest of them."

"There are times you can be such a killjoy." He

handed over the picture.

JB took it. "Go get reacquainted with you're VCR if you want to see the guy." JB looked over at him. "Len, we're going to have to do to Jenny the same thing that we did to Johnny last night. Are you all right with that?"

Len picked up his glass and swallowed the last of his gin. "I'm right behind you, Columbo."

They went upstairs to Jennifer's apartment and rang the bell. There was no answer. When JB rang a second time and got the same result, Len said, "It looks like she isn't home. What'll we do now?"

"We'll have to catch her later. How do you feel about lunch?"

"Fine. What are you in the mood for?"

"How about Italian?"

"OK. I know a place...Wait a minute. You're not thinking what I think you're thinking? JB, that's crazy. It's the real Mafia. The big guys. We could get in real trouble. Or maimed. Or killed. Or worse!"

"Len, it's a public restaurant. All we're going to do is have lunch. This isn't the nineteen thirties. Nor is it Chicago. We don't have violin cases filled with machine guns and neither do they."

"Tell that to Jimmy Hoffa. If we do this there's a good chance we'll be seeing him."

JB walked to the stairs. "You don't have to come along you know."

Len hesitated a moment, then shook his head. He started after JB who was now going down the stairs "I'll go," he said. "But if I end up in a concrete ballgown,with gravel wedgies, I'll never forgive you."

JB arrived at the bottom of the lobby stairs with Len still grousing behind him. He looked out the lobby door and spotted a familiar figure flouncing her way up the walk. He stood aside, looked at Len with a grin, and let him proceed ahead of him.

Mrs. Forsyth-Peal opened the door and stepped inside. She smiled broadly at Len, nodded imperiously toward JB, and passed them both, heading for the stairs.

Just as she reached them Len said, "How's it going, Stormy? Are your tassels still twirling in different directions?"

She stopped cold, one foot lifted toward the first step, frozen, like Lot's wife, for a good thirty seconds. Then she turned to the two men. Her face was white under the color she had painted on. She had the same look as a condemned man when taking his last mile. Her bottom lip quivered. "What kind of question is that?"

"The same as what was it like to strip three-a-day for Minsky's Burlesque?"

"Jesus-H-Cow-pocky! You know!" Her ham-like hand went to her chest and patted, which caused her right breast to shake like disturbed meringue.

JB stepped forward. "You bet we do, Stormy. And

we want to know who else knew."

Stormy lowered herself heavily to the steps and opened her purse. She began searching through it. "What in the name of my Aunt Levinia's garters are you a talkin' 'bout?"

Stormy was so upset she had forgotten to watch her speech and all vestiges of her upper class accent had disappeared. She pulled out a handkerchief and mopped her forehead. "I've spent the last twenty years a hidin' my past. Who else woulda' known?"

"How about Mrs. Lucan?"

Stormy furiously fanned herself with the damp handkerchief. "Cum-suckin' mother-fartin' diddly-squat! You know 'bout her too? I shoulda' known. The old crotch-sucker never could have kept her trap shut, even when I was all set to pay her."

"Then she was trying to blackmail you. How much were you to pay her?"

"Hon, I wasn't goin' to pay her in money. She wanted intros. To all my society friends. She was 'posed to go to that musical with me, but when she didn't show up I was mighty relieved, let me tell you."

"It sounds like she was planning on expanding her horizons, JB. To do more business."

"You got it, hoss. I tried to tell her she had 'bout as much chance as a pederast at a Boy Scout picnic of bein' accepted by those folks, but there was no arguin' her out of it. Crips, it nearly took me ten years and that was only cause I was Ham's wife."

"And the way she dressed would have raised a few eyebrows for sure."

"Hoo-ee, weren't she a sight? Looked like a two-dollar whore with only a nickel to spend. Most strippers of my acquaintance dressed better, and most a them had all their taste stuck in their mouths."

Len asked, "Where are your people from anyway?"

"Some lil' old town up in the hills of Tennessee. You would a never heard of it."

"Try me."

"It's only three shacks an' a general store. Called Muletree Hollar."

Len smiled. "Now if I recollect that's right next to Wilson's Creek, which is just over the hill from Jupiter's Crossing."

"By God, you're a down home boy! I knew I liked you for good reason. So you surely do know why'd I hide my white trash roots. Same as you do yours."

"Wait a second, Stormy. I don't hide my roots from the world. I don't make a big deal over them, but everyone know's I'm from the South."

"Whatever, hoss. You might not hide 'em, but you don't go shoutin' 'bout em' in Times Square neither. Well, I was born trash, an' in the part of the South we was raised in you know that's bein' redundant. So, I got myself away from that Hollar quick as I could. I still had to eat so I hooked up in a two-bit strip joint in the first town I came to. I did change my name so Mama wouldn't know. I was born Annie Mae Creedle. Boy, I had me some good lookin' body back then. With this terrific pair a juggs. So I started travelin' an strippin'. From clip joint to slop chute an back again. I made the big time when this fella caught my act in Nashville."

"How did you end up in New York?"

"After lot's a years a shakin' my tits, an' haten' it more an' more. Of puttin' up with dirty theaters an' dirtier managers. Of bad money an' worse women. You ever smelled a dressin' room fulla' unwashed G-strings, old greasepaint, an' BO all mixed together? It's enough to make a person think pig-shit is violets, let me tell you. So I wanted out real bad. I was workin' Boston, at the Grand Burlycue, when I met Ham. He didn't give a donkey's fart where I come from or what I did, bless his heart. An' we got hitched. His mama 'bout dropped her girdle when she first laid eyes on me. She's the one taught me to talk, an' walk, an' dress, an' all. Her baby boy married to a stripper? Well, she was gonna make a lady from me if she had to die in the process." Stormy shook her head. "She didn't, but I almost did. An' the secret just kept goin' year after year."

"And you enjoy living like that?"

"Jesus H. Fudge-packin' dip-stickers! Why do you think I'm always stuffin' myself? It don't take some high priced therapist to see why I'm miserable. Always watchin' what I say an' how I say it. An' I hate those tight-ass snobs we run with. An' I hate bein' as fat as an old sow. But life is choices, an' I chose Ham. This here is his world."

"But you also said he didn't care where you came from or what you did," JB said.

"But those friends of his do. They'd drop me like a sheepherder at a Texas barbecue if they found out 'bout my past. Please don't say anything. If not for me then for Ham."

Len sat beside Stormy on the steps. "I can promise I won't. JB won't either. But you need to take a look at what you've become. You really need to loosen up, Annie Mae. If Ham really loves you he won't care how his friends think about you. In fact, he still loves you with all this weight, right?"

Len took her pudgy hand in his and held it.

JB said, "You know, what you did for a living or what you had to do to keep yourself alive has little or nothing to do with what kind of person you are. Underneath all that Victorian playacting you do there is a genuine and loving person. The person Ham fell for in the beginning."

"I'll bet there's a lot of spunk in there too," Len added.

"You dragged yourself up from the worst kind of beginnings. You deserve to bring that survivor out and see what it's like to be your real self. You might find out it's more fun. And those friends of yours might like her too."

Len leaned over to her. "Personally, I think you're a ten gallon hoot."

She looked at her ample lap for a moment. Then her face took on that Southern stubborn look that still thinks it could win against the Yankees. She slapped her thigh.

"You know what?" she said. "You might be right. Me pretendin' to be somethin' I'm not is like dressin' up a nanny goat in spangles an' callin' it Miss America. I am what I am, as the wolf said after eatin' a lamb chop. At least I can try to be myself from now on."

Len smiled. "That's the idea. But I think Jerry Herman wrote *I Am What I Am*."

"Lord-a-mighty, I didn't know he was Southern!" Stormy threw back her head and laughed a laugh from deep inside. It was loud, raucous, and the harbinger of quite a character to be. Her laugh stopped abruptly. "You know those people are sure to care 'bout my past. They really are snobbyier than snobs. They're so bad they don't even like themselves most of the time."

"Well, you'll just have to go out and find another set of friends. You can start with JB and me."

She pulled Len to her and kissed his cheek. Then she reached for JB and did the same. "Thank you, both. It hasn't been much fun these last years. But if I lose me 'bout a thousand pounds I'll bet you I can still shake a pretty mean tassel." She laughed again and then started up the stairs.

JB looked over at Len who was watching Stormy go up. "Well, you really zapped her didn't you, you old softy."

"Give me a break. I ended up feeling sorry for her. So, I'm a mensch."

"You are, Len. A bonafide A-number-one Southern fried mensch." Who it couldn't hurt to follow the same advice he just handed out so freely, JB added to himself.

The cab pulled up in front of the Cie Bella restaurant in Little Italy. "Are you sure you want to do this?"

"Yes." JB reached over to open the car door. Len followed him out of the car

"We could get pizza instead, JB I'll even let you have it with pepperoni if we must. There's a parlor right across the street. Right there." Len pointed in that direction.

"Will you stop it? Come on." JB left him standing in the street and went inside the restaurant.

The same traveling band of interior decorators had done every Italian eating place in America. The restaurant had red checked tablecloths, wine bottles with candles, breadsticks stuck in drinking glasses, and *Arrivaderci Roma* playing softly in the background. Along one wall were booths, all empty. Of the ten tables in the center there was only one filled by a young man and his girlfriend. At the rear of the restaurant was a swinging door with a round porthole window at the top.

Len came up beside JB. "This isn't so bad."

"What did you expect? Gun racks in the checkroom?"

"OK. So I overreacted."

They sat at a table. A few minutes later a waiter came from the back carrying two glasses of water. He set them down, greeted them, and told them the day's specials. They ordered and the waiter returned to the rear. In five minutes he was back, put their plates of food down, wished them good appetites, and left.

"Hey, I have to admit the service is great," Len said. He took a bite of his ravioli. "And this is really good. How's yours?"

JB was going to answer when the front door flew open. In walked a large dark-haired hulk of a man. He was followed by another slightly smaller hulk that had short crewcut blond hair. Both wore wraparound sunglasses that hid the majority of their faces. The blond looked around, nodded, and stepped aside. Then Vincent Gallentini entered and walked the length of the restaurant to the farthest rear booth. He sat facing the front door while the two guards took a table directly across from his booth. The waiter appeared at Gallentini's table faster than he had served Len and JB.

JB watched this entrance as he held a forkful of food midway between his plate and his mouth. This has got to be the way Al Capone entered a place during the twenties, he thought. It's nice that mobsters still respect their traditions. But then a basic survival instinct would do that wouldn't it?

Len had hunched down in his seat and was staring at a pool of tomato sauce on his plate. Without looking up he whispered to JB, "That blond guard. That's the guy we thought was the cleaning boy. What's he doing here?"

JB put the chunk of Veal Parmesan on his fork into his mouth and swallowed. "I don't know, Len. Maybe apartment cleaning doesn't pay enough so he took a part time job as a mobster."

"Very funny."

"What it really means is Gallentini has some connection to your building or his bodyguard wouldn't have been there. We have to find out what the connection is."

"And how are we to do that? I don't think going up and asking for his autograph as an ice breaker is going to work."

"Well let's finish our lunch. Maybe we'll think of something." JB continued to eat.

Len, however, kept looking up and down between his plate, Gallentini, the two guards, the front door, and JB. If he were at a tennis match he wouldn't look out of place. Here he stuck out like a teenager at a nudist camp.

Gallentini, meanwhile, had called over the buzz-cut blond bodyguard to his booth. A moment later the guard walked the length of the room toward JB and Len.

"Len, stop it. You're drawing attention to us."

"I can't help it, JB. Where's the bathroom?"

"Well, why didn't you say so? It's probably over there."

Len stood and found himself face to chest with the blond bodyguard. He slowly sank back into his chair and looked up. The guard smiled down at him. "Hello again," he said. "Did you finally get your place cleaned?" Len nodded mutely. Then without turning away from Len, Blondie said to JB, "My boss wants to see you. Back there." He jerked his thumb in the direction of the booth.

JB swallowed a large lump of food that had stuck in his throat, got up and went toward the rear of the restaurant. Blondie sat down across from Len and lowered the sunglasses on his nose.

Gallentini looked up with hooded dark eyes that for some reason JB found eerily familiar. Where had he seen them before? The sharpened senses he had clicked on for this meeting with a real in-the-flesh mobster made it impossible to think beyond the here and now. His memory circuits had gone temporarily out of order. Gallentini nodded a greeting and held out his hand. Am I supposed to shake it or kiss it?, JB thought. He decided to shake it very carefully.

Gallentini's voice was soft and carried an authority in it. He was used to getting his own way. "You're Jeremy Bent, the mystery writer. I've read a couple of your books. They're good. Sit down. Have some wine. We'll talk."

JB sat. The Mafia don poured a glass of wine and slid it across the table. The dark-haired bodyguard slid into the booth next to JB.

"I especially liked the first book," Gallentini continued. "The one that received an award. I couldn't figure out who the killer was. For me that's the sign of a good mystery."

"Thank you," JB said. "I'm glad you liked it. Do you read a lot of mysteries, Mr. Gallentini?"

"Ah, you know who I am then. Good. Yes, I read Christie, Chandler, Hammett. I like mysteries. Which brings me to my question, Mr. Bent. Why are you here in Little Italy?"

JB thought, think fast. A life might depend on it. Mine! But he said, "Research, Mr. Gallentini. For a new book I have planned."

Gallentini leaned forward, put his elbows on the table and his chin in his hands. "Really? A new mystery? What's it about?"

Oh, God. You couldn't have just said you were here for lunch now could you?, JB thought.

"Uh, it is a mystery..." JB said. The sentence sat there for a long moment, then as the silence thickened, JB continued. "...about a young boy who goes bad and ends up in jail. There are several chapters about his experiences in the joint. The hierarchy of the prisoners, guys putting the make on him. That sort of thing." Hey, this isn't bad, JB thought. "Then the boy gets caught up in an escape. Once he's out he heads for New York. He figures he can get lost in the crowds here," he finished. Where is this coming from?

"Fascinating," Gallentini said. "But where does Little Italy come in?"

"Well...Uh...The boy gets hooked up with an underground surgeon who does plastic surgery to change his face and destroy his fingerprints." Now that's a slice of real life isn't it? "So, the boy needs a place to stay....to recuperate....and he contacts the head of an Italian mob family...who has....a place......for him to hide ou...."

Gallentini's face grew hard, as his eyes became pinpointed laser beams. Aimed directly at JB.

JB's thoughts screamed at him. Jesus! You've gone too far. This man has absolutely no sense of irony.

Gallentini slammed both hands on the table. His face was angry.

No sense of humor either.

"Very interesting concept, Mr. Bent. This book of yours is fiction, right? And only a planned book at this point?"

JB could understand why they called Gallentini "Iceman". The temperature in the booth had dropped about thirty degrees. The perspiration on his forehead felt like ice cubes. JB stammered, "Of co...course."

"Good. Because you probably couldn't afford the consequences of writing such a book, Mr. Bent."

The Mafioso flicked his eyelids and JB felt the bodyguard next to him grab onto his thigh. He was pretty sure that it wasn't a pass. The grip on his leg got tighter and more painful as Gallentini continued. "Being of Italian decent, and having buildings all over the city, I could easily take offense at the sort of portrayal you plan. Of course, I am only a real estate man and not a mobster, so it couldn't be me you are writing about. Could it, Mr. Bent?"

JB felt the hand leave his thigh. A second later the guard's fist pounded. Once. Hard. On his testicles. JB leaned foreword onto the table as a blinding pain seared through his body and exploded inside his head. His eyes filled with tears as he uttered an agonized moan.

The guard took hold of a handful of JB's hair and pulled him back to a sitting position facing Gallentini. Through watery vision JB could see a thin smile play on the man's face. His eyes, however, were still as frosty as an Arctic iceflow.

"What's going on here?"

All three faces in the booth turned. Len was standing outside the booth. "You've been gone quiet awhile, JB."

Gallentini said in a voice as smooth as a knife's edge, "We won't be much longer. Won't you join us?"

Len shook his head. "No. Thank you. I'll just go back to our tab..."

The blond bodyguard stepped up behind Len and put his hand on his shoulder. "The boss wants you should sit." Len was pushed down into the booth next to the dark haired guard.

"Well, if you insist...Hey!" Len turned to the guard sitting next to him. The guards right hand was gripping Len's thigh. JB shook his head. Len, finally seeing the fear and pain on JB's face, decided to shut up. For once he did the right thing.

Gallentini looked at JB and signaled again with his eyelids. The dark-haired guard flung his arms around JB's and Len's necks. He then pulled them close to him so their heads rested in his armpits. He was holding them like they were teddy bears won on a carnival midway.

The blond guard, still standing beside the booth, took out a nine millimeter Beretta and pointed it level with Len's temple.

Gallentini said, "You would like a book plot, Mr. Bent? Listen to this. Maybe you can use it. A nosy writer keeps asking too many questions of the wrong people, so that he and his friend end up hanging from a meat hook in a slaughter house I own over near West Fourth. It isn't pretty, Mr. Bent, if you understand my meaning."

"Why don't you let the two men leave, Gallentini?"

Gallentini turned toward the voice and saw a young man standing, legs apart, aiming a large Smith and Wesson police pistol straight at him. Beside him, in a crouch, was a young woman also holding a revolver.

"Officer Dehil, NYPD. This is my partner, Officer Jakes." The man and his girlfriend, who sat having a quiet meal when JB and Len came in, were cops.

"We've been watching you, Gallentini. Along with the Feds. You don't want to be arrested for the harassment of a private citizen, now would you? That's much too penny-ante for you."

Gallentini smiled. "We were just talking literature, officer. You read any good books lately?"

"Yeah. *The Godfather*. I like to know what I'm dealing with. Now, drop the gun, Blondie." The automatic clattered on the tile floor. Blondie had his hands up.

"You want to let the two men go on their way now don't you, Gallentini?"

"Of course. Step aside. Let them out." He waved a hand. The blond took a step back, Len got up, the dark haired guard slid out, and JB followed.

"Thank you, Officer."

Gallentini drummed his fingers on the table, drawing JB's attention back to him. "It was a pleasure, Mr. Bent. I hope you'll remember the plot I told you."

JB and Len went to their table, left money to pay for their mostly uneaten meals, and scurried out of the restaurant.

They jumped into the first cab that stopped and directed the driver out of Little Italy. When they were a few blocks away JB began to breathe a bit easier.

"Thank God we're out of there, JB. You looked pretty scared back there."

"You heard what he said. And that bodyguard tried to do a sex change operation on me without benefit of surgical instruments."

"Do you think Gallentini is serious?"

"Len, the man has no sense of whimsy. We were being threatened not being asked to a debutante's cotillion."

"Really? That blond bodyguard asked me for a date. But that was for his sister's wedding next Saturday."

JB looked over at Len. Then he started to laugh. Slowly at first then he began to pick up speed. JB's laughter was vigorous and slightly forced and betrayed an edge sharp with hysteria. Len looked perplexed but soon joined in. They laughed together until their sides hurt.

L en opened the door to his apartment, picked up the flyer that had been shoved under it, and crumpled it. "Chinese menus," he said. "Everyday there's another one. I think there must be hordes of tiny oriental gnomes in collie hats running up and down the halls of all the apartment buildings in Manhattan." He pitched the menu ball in the direction of the kitchen.

JB went behind the ball in the same direction. "Actually they bring the flyers when they deliver an order in a building."

"Not nearly as romantic as my version, JB. Hey, what's up? You don't look at all cheerful."

JB had sat at the table and indeed had an if not grim then very dark look on his face. "This whole murder thing is finally getting to me, Len. So far I've been warned out of it by overzealous cops, beat up by drug pushers, scared out of my wits by an alleged bimbo, condescended to by a corn-pone ex-stripper, yelled at by a B-movie gangster, and now, practically neutered and threatened with my life by mobsters. This has not exactly been a cabaret, old chum."

"I guess you're right. When put that way it does sound like a Sondheim musical plotline. So you'll quit the case?"

"No, Len, I won't. Because I keep feeling like we're right on the edge of finding out who did this."

"But, JB, we haven't eliminated any of the suspects. In fact we picked up a couple on the way."

"Helmut Lucan's gone. He has an airtight alibi according to Kelly."

"However, there is still the mysterious sister who doesn't exist. And then Hackshaw. And now Gallentini."

"I suppose. But Hackshaw's really out of the running I think. He's like a dog and won't crap, or crime, where he sleeps. And Gallentini seems pretty busy with the cops and the Feds to worry about some old woman and her petty blackmail scheme. I still don't know what his tie to this is."

"What about the boys? I certainly don't trust them. What if that club manager lied? How could he be so sure the boys were there? I can't keep track of people in those places."

"Then there's Johnny."

"He was in Ohio."

"But it is possible he could have flown here, killed her, and still have had enough time to get back to Ohio for a flight to New York later that evening.

And what about Stormy? She could have killed her, but why would she have brought her downstairs to your apartment. That doesn't seem likely given her weight. There is the old man."

"JB, if he had killed Mrs. Lucan it probably would have taken him a couple of days just to get the body across the hall. He's so frail and weak he has trouble lifting one of those books he has over there in his apartment."

"I've heard that people can come up with tremendous strength in emergency situations, and having just killed someone would cause a major degree of panic I'll bet. So he's still a possibility, a remote one for sure, but still there. He had opportunity."

"And Stormy did say that Mrs. Lucan didn't show up for that musical she was supposed to go to. That started around nine. Where was Mrs. Lucan between then and two A.M. when she was killed?"

"And dressed in that nightgown. Maybe the lady next door can shed some light on the question.

"So we still have to talk to Jennifer, right?"

JB picked up the envelope of pictures. "Yeah, we do. But get out your hip boots. Here we go stomping around in someone's private life again."

When Jennifer responded to JB's and Len's knock on her door she was wearing a filmy pale green chiffon negligee. It seemed like overkill at three in the afternoon. She blinked her Bambi-like eyes rapidly and asked what they wanted.

JB said, "We have a few more questions to ask, Jennifer. Could you take the time? It's important."

She fidgeted a bit, the ostrich feathers on the cuffs of her robe wafting and waving from the movement. "Well, I was kinda...No...It's all right. Come on in." She turned and crossed the room. A single feather was left behind to float leisurely to the floor. She settled on the sofa with her legs pulled up. Len again sat opposite. JB remained standing.

JB looked directly at Jennifer. "What I was wondering about was if you were aware that Mrs. Lucan was blackmailing your boyfriend?"

Len slid down in his chair. "Nothing like getting right to the point. Subtle, JB. Real subtle."

"I'm sick and tired of subtle, Len. Let's get this affair settled."

"Oh, and that's real subtle too."

Jennifer's eyes were open wide and blinking. "I don't understand." She gave them a bewildered look.

JB spoke gruffly. "Cut the bimbo act, Jennifer. Enough already." He looked around the room. "And you can get your boyfriend out here too. Where is he? In the bedroom?"

Her eyes lost their saucer like quality. The previously luscious lips pulled into a thin line. She ran a hand through her hair. "Damn it! I've been making people think I'm something I'm not for years. I can usually fool any man with that dumb Dora act."

Len said, "But not a gay man, sweetheart. We invented the game of hiding what we are."

Jennifer turned her head toward the bedroom and called out. "Andy!"

The bedroom door opened and a sheepish Andrew Whitlow walked across the room and sat next to Jennifer. "How did you know I was here?"

"Jennifer isn't exactly dressed for the ladies auxiliary is she?" JB waved a hand in the air. "Plus, Jennifer doesn't smoke and this place reeks of tobacco. That you were actually still here was a lucky guess."

"I told you to stop smoking," Jennifer scolded.

"All right Jenny." Whitlow patted her on the thigh. "Jenny told me about you two questioning her.

I thought you had been warned."

"That's how Kelly knew what we had done. You pulled strings and had us warned to stop, right?"

"One of the perks of being in the city government. So why are you still sticking your nose in where it doesn't belong?"

JB sat on the arm of Len's chair. "My friend here is the main suspect in this murder. Your affair with Jennifer isn't going to be responsible for him spending the rest of his days in a jail cell. No matter how sordid the papers could turn it into it isn't worth ruining another man's life to keep it secret."

"He's right, Andy." Jennifer took hold of the hand still resting on her thigh. He used his other hand to pat hers. "All right. What do you want?"

JB pulled Mrs. Lucan's photos of the two of them out of the envelope and handed them to Whitlow. He took them gingerly, scanned them, and then looked up. "So the noble speech was just a scam, huh? This is the same old business with new owners. How much do you want?"

JB's voice grew hard. "Stuff it, Whitlow. You can keep your dirty little secret. I don't want anything from you but information." He reached into the envelope and pulled out the negatives to the pictures. He threw them at Whitlow.

"I'm sorry. It's just that....Well, its like that old saying. Once burned, twice shy."

"More like, you lay down with dogs, you get up with fleas," Len said.

"I guess you're right. If there wasn't anything to hide I wouldn't have to pay the blackmail."

"So, Whitlow, how long did you have to pay?"

"All of last year. To the tune of something like sixty-five thousand dollars."

JB whistled.

"That's not a tune, that's a friggin' aria," Len said.

"What happened?" JB stood over Whitlow. "Did you get tired of paying out and kill her?"

Whitlow sounded shocked. "No! A man in my position couldn't chance something like that. I may do adultery, but murder....No way."

Jennifer added, " I wasn't lying to you the other day. Andy and I were together. Here. All night."

"With only each other as witnesses. Wouldn't stand up to a strong judge in a slow wind, Jennifer. You could have helped him do it."

"I know it doesn't look very good but you have to believe us. We didn't kill her. Mrs. Lucan wasn't even in her apartment that night. How could we have killed her if she wasn't even there?"

"What's do you mean, Jennifer?"

"Andy and I were having drinks here on the couch around nine P.M. I heard her door open and then I heard her go down the stairs. We stayed up until almost three and I never heard her come back."

"How could you be sure it was her that left?"

"She wore spring-a-lators all the time. You know high heels with no backs on them. They make a noise that is pretty easy to identify. I always heard her clip-clopping around. Please, JB. Please Len, you've got to believe me." She began to cry.

Whitlow put his arms around her. "I remember Jenny saying something to me about Mrs. Lucan going out that night. I didn't think much about it then. Listen, I admit I hated the old woman. I'll even admit I tried to think of a way to get out of paying her. But that's all. I couldn't kill her. It would destroy everything I've ever worked for."

"So could this situation with Jennifer if it ever got out. You lucked out this time. With Mrs. Lucan dead you would seem to be off the hook. And, call me crazy, but I believe you both. Jennifer maybe more than you, but until there's some evidence to prove me wrong I don't think you killed her. Come on, Len. Let's go."

They walked to the door and left Jennifer and Whitlow to decide their futures together, or apart.

Back in Len's apartment JB sat at the kitchen table and opened Mrs. Lucan's notebook. Len went to the cabinet and pulled out the makings of his favorite drink. A bottle of gin. JB flipped to the right page of the notebook and crossed off 'Bombay Season' from the list.

"There's three left. And it could still be any one of the eight. Hell, it might be anyone within the boundaries of New York City. Even me. Everyone's got something they don't want the world to know about."

Len sat across from JB with his full to the brim glass of gin. "I don't get why she didn't try to blackmail me. God knows I have secrets. I'm gay for one thing. I must be on that list."

"Who says you're not? You're Lord Snowy-White."

"I am? Damn! Wait. I don't get it."

"It's easy once you get how Mrs. Lucan's mind worked. Now, pay attention. What gets your clothes clean and snowy white?"

"You've been watching way to much TV, JB." He looked steadily at Len. "OK. Soap. Satisfied?"

"Right. And what part did you play on your soap opera?"

Len sighed. He had said this a thousand times or more. "Lord Percival Hawthorne."

JB snapped his fingers. "Lord Snowy-White. Do you get it?"

Len laughed. "Got it. But why didn't she hit on me, JB?"

JB bit his lower lip. He handed the notebook over to Len. "Look at what she's written about you." JB sat back as Len read the entry. It said: *Lord doesn't like a Lady—Not enough. The downing could be.* Written below that in red ink was: *No good. Crier has told all.*

Len looked up. "What does she mean, Mr. Moto?"

"Ancient proverb say, keep hole shut and listen." JB took a deep breath and plunged ahead. "Mrs. Lucan is referring, at first, to the fact that you're gay. But that isn't enough for blackmail. This is New York after all. I mean most of the industry knows your sexual proclivity. Then, she thinks your drinking will do it. She gave up that idea when the criers, or the tabloids, printed all those sordid stories about you and your escapades while drunk. Remember? Not very pretty, Len."

JB stopped for a moment, now he was up to the hard part.

"Len, I hope you know how much I love you. So, I'll do this one more time. You are my best friend, and I can't stand watching you ruin your life and your career by the amount of drinking you do."

"What are you talking about, JB? My career is fine. In fact, I have an audition next week."

"Pull another one of the stunts like you pulled at the last audition you showed up for and you'll be completely blackballed from the entire business. Literally pissing on a script is not considered acceptable behavior, Len, even if it really is a bad script. If you walk in tanked again, like you did at those last six auditions you won't even be let in the door. You used to gripe that typecasting lost you parts. That's bullshit, Len. Your being drunk on your ass lost you those parts. Show business is a hotbed of gossip. Len, you have a reputation. And it isn't for being humanitarian of the year."

"Stop it," Len said.

"And what about your other friends? The few you have left of all the ones you've insulted so often that they finally dropped you. And you, Len? You're killing yourself. The slow hard way, one drink at a time. You know how it goes. First your liver will stop cleaning out the daily intake of booze, and then your mind will decide to give it up. Have you ever seen a person with wet brain, Len? Damaged beyond repair by alcohol. I can take you to the flight deck at Bellevue if you want to see one in person. Or, you can wait a few years and just look in the mirror."

Len spoke louder. "Stop it."

"You do know that your drinking is the main reason you and I had to break up? I couldn't stand by and watch you destroy yourself. And you wanted your booze more than you wanted to be with me. Len, please, you have to stop. There are ways. You can get help. You have a disease. Its called alcoholism."

Len stood up from his chair and leaned his hands on the table. His face red with anger, he screamed at JB. "Get out! Get out of here, JB! Before I hurt you! I mean it. I don't want to hear anymore! Get out!"

JB, in as soft a voice as he was able to muster, said, "All right, Len. But think about what I've said." He stood and went to the door. He hesitated, then he left.

Len, still standing at the table, shouted to no one, or maybe to himself. "I hate you! I hate you! I hate you!" Then he sat and let the tears run down his face. He reached for the glass of gin he left on the table and with a trembling hand brought it to his mouth. As he drank, he continued to cry.

At the bottom of the lobby stairs JB spotted Toby locking the door to apartment 1-A. "The boy's are gone," Toby said

"Huh" JB answered.

Toby looked up and pointed to the outside door. Kenny and Blondel were standing on the sidewalk surrounded by cardboard boxes of their belongings. As JB and Toby watched, Kenny laid his hand on Blondel's back. Blondel angrily pulled away and turned on Kenny. He yelled then put both hands on Kenny's chest and shoved. Kenny stepped back, lost his balance, and fell into the center of their boxes. Blondel started gesticulating wildly.

JB shook his head. "As Gertrude Stein was known to have said...A homophobe is a homophobe is a homophobe."

"They didn't have very much left to pack after this mornings fight. Now they don't need to take anything."

Toby turned to look at JB. His eyes were showing a sadness and hurt that caused Toby real concern. "What's wrong, JB? You look like you've lost your best friend. Has something happened to Len?"

"As cliché as that sounds it isn't very far from the truth. I may have." JB explained what happened after he left Toby that morning. When he was finished he sat on the bottom step of the stairs. "I just hope Len heard a little of what I said. He has to get some help."

Toby sat beside him. "JB, you can't drag Len to a rehab. He has to go on his own."

"I know all that. But it doesn't make it any easier. How do I stand by and watch him destroy himself. Every day he gets a bit worse. He goes a little more out of control. He can't get work, so he drinks more. Without his career he thinks he's a big nothing. That's how he thinks. So he has two choices. Kill himself or keep drinking. And the second choice is the same as the first. I don't know what to do."

JB couldn't say anymore. If he said another word all his control would be gone and then he'd start crying. And he wasn't sure he could ever stop the tears again. His fists clenched on his thighs and he pushed down. Hard. "No. Damn it, I've cried enough for Len. No more." He squared his shoulders and wiped his face with the back of his hand. "Well, at least the morning wasn't a total loss. We crossed four people off of Mrs. Lucan's list."

"Wow. That's a lot. Who's left?"

"There's Super Wine and Berlin Assurance.

But who they could be is anyone's guess."

"If the other six names were people in this building it would seem like she followed a pattern. Who's left here? What about the Professor?"

"Well, the Professor is German. That could explain Berlin. But the Assurance part doesn't make sense. And that only leaves 'Super Wine'. What that has to do with a Mafia don, I haven't a clue. And the Mafia part doesn't jibe with your pattern theory."

"A Mafia don?" Toby looked away.

"Yeah. Among Mrs. Lucan's pictures there was one of a Mafia capo standing in that doorway..." JB pointed to the lobby door. "...talking to someone here. Len thinks he was supplying drugs to the two boys. I think it was something else. Toby, what's the story on apartment 4-B?"

"It's what I told the police earlier. The place is rented by an agency for their clients. The agent comes by and lets me know when someone is moving in. I get the place cleaned and the clients stay for however long they need to. Usually I don't even see them." Toby still hasn't looked over at JB.

"That's what happened with Hackshaw?"

"Yeah."

"And the agent is a big blond guy with a buzz-cut and sunglasses." Toby now turned to look at JB. He nodded. "Then I have to be right. This building is a hide-out for crooks on the lam."

"What?"

"Sorry, Toby. I know this has been a rotten few days for you, but there's something else. It looks like Vincent Gallentini is renting apartment 4-B as a place to hide escaped criminals. It probably started way before you got here if that will make it easier to explain to your boss."

"Gallentini was the guy in the pictures then?" Toby hesitated a moment and then asked the next question. "Who was he talking too?"

"Actually, we couldn't tell, except that it was a male. He was inside the lobby and it shadowed his face."

Toby and JB sat silently for a moment.

"I was just thinking," JB said. "In England aren't insurance companies called assurance companies? If that's the case then maybe the Professor is 'Berlin Assurance'. You said that Mrs. Lucan was always flirting with him. What if the plan was to marry him, then get rid of him, and collect his insurance?"

"Kinda crazy. After all, the man is over seventy and he hasn't been married. He's probably gay, so why would he marry her. And doesn't assurance also mean to make someone sure of something? Like self confidence?"

"Yes, it does. But that description doesn't fit the Professor or the notes."

"What do the notes say?"

"Something nonsensical. It says, *German Herr wears hosen.* Which is about as clear as mud. Let's see Herr is German for man or mister and hosen are socks. Most men wear socks, right? So we're right back at that brick wall."

"You really get off on this, don't you, JB?"

"What I like is puzzle solving. This I hate. Having to muck around in other people's private places, exposing their secrets. Secrets are filthy. People die from them."

"Die? I don't understand?"

"How about Mrs. Lucan? Secrets killed her. Or her discovery of them sure did. Secrets are dangerous. I had an uncle. His secret killed him. Uncle Bill was in the Army during Korea. He also was a closeted gay man. Men had to be in closets back then. When one of Uncle Bill's buddies was caught with another man he named names to save his own skin. Uncle Bill's was one of the names. Uncle Bill hung himself in his barracks rather than have that secret exposed.

Of course, my family never talked about it. So, we have a secret on top of a secret. It's never-ending."

"That's awful, JB. It must have been terrible to be gay back then," Toby said. "I'm glad it's easier today."

"Maybe here in a big city, but out in the smaller towns, like in Kansas, where I was raised, it isn't so easy…"

JB paused, letting an idea germinate and take form. "Toby, can I see you later? I have to go talk to someone."

"Sure. But, who?"

"A friend of mine. He's in the Army."

JB knocked on the apartment door.

He had made his call and his Army friend had confirmed what JB had figured out. That had necessitated another call. This time a long distance call to another military friend in Washington DC.

Now JB stood waiting for an answer to his knock. There was none.

"Come on," JB said. "I know you're in there."

He reached for the doorbell with the card above it and pushed the button. He heard the chimes and then, finally, there was some movement from inside.

"Now, vhat is it you want, young man?" Professor VonWettering sat back in his chair. He was wearing the same suit as before but it was baggier and hung looser on his body than two days ago. He looked pale and seemed older, if that was possible. "I've been having a nausea attack today. Please be brief," he said..

"I'm sorry you're not well, Professor. Perhaps you should see a doctor?"

"I don't trust them. They are all fakes. I haven't seen a medical doctor in my whole life. Except when I went for my hearing aid. My people believed in holistic methods. They have served me well."

He reached over to the small table beside his chair. It was piled with the usual books and papers, along with a gold fountain pen, an old-fashioned heavy metal slide rule, and a glass filled with a brownish liquid. He picked up the glass, drank most of the liquid and set it back down.

"That should take care of it." He burped daintily. "So, you have questions?"

"Yes sir, about Mrs. Lucan. She visited you the night she died, didn't she?"

"I told you before that I didn't see her."

"No, sir, that isn't exactly right. You told me you didn't hear anything. With your hearing aid turned down I'm sure you didn't. But you did see Mrs. Lucan. She left her apartment before nine that evening dressed in her nightgown and came here. For some reason known only to her she had decided to come here instead of going with Mrs. Forsyth-Peal. You let her in, Professor. What for? She was a blackmailer. Did she find out something about you? Some secret you didn't want known? Perhaps that you had gone AWOL from the military during the war?"

"Vhat are you talking about, young man? You're all vrong. I vasn't in the var. They vouldn't take me because I am German."

"No, Professor, that isn't what they did in that war. You would have been drafted just the same as any other twenty-five year old in 1942. But you wouldn't have had to fight your own people. You would have been sent to the Pacific action, Professor, not Germany. So, you didn't serve. Why, Professor? Did you go AWOL, as I suspect? Or was your secret that you're a transvestite? In fact, you're the one who came to Mrs. Lucan's apartment pretending to be her deaf sister. The gold pen the sister used to make her notes is lying right there on your table. It not good to leave evidence in plain sight, Professor."

He started to speak.

JB stopped him. "It doesn't matter, Professor. I have a friend in Washington. He's checking out the AWOL thing. I'll know by tomorrow. But that's why you killed Mrs. Lucan, isn't it, Professor? She found out this dark secret you've kept hidden all these years?"

The old man's face went a sickly white. His hands were trembling. He reached over to the table and grabbed at the metal slide rule. He stood and with a speed that belied his age he advanced on JB. "It vill stay hidden until I die!" He held the slide rule aloft as a weapon.

JB stood where he was, stunned, as the old man stepped toward him. Then VonWettering stopped. The slide rule dropped to the floor and he clutched at his chest. He groaned as his eyes rolled up leaving only the whites showing. He crumpled to the floor.

JB rushed to him and touched his neck. He found a weak pulse. He grabbed the phone, dialed 911 and gave the information they asked for, then returned to the old man. He checked again for a pulse but couldn't find one. He quickly tilted VonWettering's head back, pinched his nostrils, and kissed him as he breathed air into his mouth.

The paramedics arrived fifteen minutes later.

"It was a heart attack, I think," JB told one of them. "He wasn't breathing. I gave him mouth to mouth until he was able to breathe on his own. He's been like that for about ten minutes."

VonWettering was alive but his breathing was shallow and erratic. The other medic bent beside him. He nodded at his partner and began to loosen the Professor's clothing. The medic standing with JB said, "You did OK. Probably saved the man's life. Who was the old guy?"

"A retired Professor," JB said. "We were talking about secrets. He got upset. That's what caused the attack."

"Tom, come look at this," the medic attending the Professor called. He went over to the Professor. He bent and looked at what his partner pointed out. He looked over at JB. "You say you were talking about secrets?"

"That's right."

"Well, this one had a doozie. This is a woman."

"You mean he's wearing women's underwear. I thought he might be a transvestite."

"No, sir. I mean this is really a female!"

"Then I was still right. I just had the vice reversed."

Hospital nurses and orderlies passed in front of JB as he waited for word on Professor Von-Wettering. He heard the elevator doors at the end of the hall open and looked up. Toby stepped out, his eyes searching one way and the other. JB stood and Toby saw him. He walked toward him.

Damn, JB thought. That is one handsome man. He's intelligent, talented, energetic, and even funny. He's just so young. Oh, stop it, JB. You're not all that old. And what does it matter anyway? If he doesn't care then why should you? Maybe it can work. I am certainly falling for him.

When Toby was a few feet away he smiled. JB smiled back.

Amend that, JB thought. You haven't fallen. You've crashed. He felt his heart beat a little faster at the realization. I'm in love with him, JB decided.

"Hi." Toby sat down next to JB. "The police were at the building again. They told me they had the paramedics bring the old man here. He's the murderer?"

JB nodded. "The main tip off was when it occurred to me that he was the only one who didn't react when he found out Mrs. Lucan wasn't a suicide. All the others did. But wait until you hear the kicker!"

JB told him what had happened. "...so that was the secret. The Professor was really a woman but had lived more than forty years dressing as a man."

"You're kidding. And that's why Mrs. Lucan was killed? Because she found out the Professor was cross dressing?"

"I thought it was something else at first. But it turned out I was wrong. How could I have guessed that when no one else had for all those years? That's a hell of a secret to keep, isn't it? It eventually led to murder."

Toby looked down at his hands. "JB, I can't keep this to myself any more. I've got to tell you something."

"That you're Super Wine?"

"You know!"

"The process of elimination certainly worked in my favor. You said it yourself. You thought that Mrs. Lucan had a pattern in her notes. If that was true then it had to be someone in the building. All the others were accounted for. You were the only one left. It was obvious then. The Super was your job, and Ernest and Julio make California wine. Once Gallo finally made sense the notes gave me the rest."

"My first name is really Anthony."

"And the last is Gallentini?"

Toby nodded.

"Is the 'Iceman' an uncle or your father?"

"My father."

"Ah, your *da*...it was dad, right?" JB smiled. "So, your father is a Mafia capo. I would hope the sins of the father don't always have to reflect on the son."

"My mother left him when I was small. I didn't even know him until a couple of years ago. When I came to New York. He had kept tabs on me over the years and when I came here he contacted me. That's when he gave me the job as the super. When I found out who he really was I changed my name."

"Toby, it really doesn't matter to me." JB took his hand. "I want to give you an answer to that question you asked me the other night." Toby looked over at him. JB took a breath. "What you and your talents will get you is a fairly well preserved mystery writer who, it turns out, cares a great deal about you and would like to go on seeing you. To see if maybe we couldn't build a relationship together. If that's what you want?"

"Yes! Of course, yes!"

Toby hugged JB. The business of the hospital continued without noticing the two men wrapped in each other's arms. That is except for one of the orderlies who did notice and decided to take home a bunch of flowers to his lover, Ralph, when he got off shift.

The doctor came to the door of VonWettering's room and motioned JB inside. He stood and entered.

The Professor was in bed hooked up to an

IV, a heart monitor, and several other machines that flashed little lights and whirred softly in the quiet of the unit.

She looked pale and wan but was awake. She turned her head when JB came near. In a soft wavery voice she thanked JB for keeping her alive.

JB nodded and asked, "Professor, I have to know. Why did you dress as a man for so long? How did it all start? And when?"

"Do you know vhat it vas like to be a voman vith a brain in 1934?" The voice was only a whisper. JB leaned in to hear her better. "It vas not like today. Vomen vere alvays stupid, even those vhen they veren't. The men who ran the vorld couldn't....No, they vouldn't let a mere voman be anything else. I vatched my mother destroyed by this system. She vas an exceptionally talented voman. An artist. But she vasn't allowed to get schooling to learn to use her gifts. Instead she vas married off to a monster. My father. He vorked her like a slave, he beat her, he broke her. I vatched her lose herself until....until she couldn't go on. She died, in my seventeenth year, by her own hand. I couldn't live like that. Vith that kind of oppression. I vouldn't let men do to me vhat they had done to her. To escape my homeland I dressed as a man. I vas accepted vithout question. It vas easy to change female to male on my papers. A difference of only two letters. Once in America I seldom vore vomen's clothes again. Their vere occasions. Once, in 1942, vhen I got my draft notice. They apologized profusely for thinking I vas a man. The fools. I've never regretted it. Any of it. I built a career no voman of my time could have. A career many men envied."

"You should be very proud, Professor." JB smiled gently. "Professor, I have to ask about Mrs. Lucan."

Her voice had faded. The words came slowly, with long stretches in between sentences.

"You vere right, young man....I killed her....
She came down that night....To cure me, she
said....That afternoon she had found my few pieces of vomen's clothing in my closet.....Vhat a silly
voman....I invited her for dinner....I vas going to
poison her.....Before ve could eat she tried to se-
duce me.......Ve grappled......she tore my shirt.......
She discovered my secret........I grabbed the first
thing I could find......My slide rule........I hit her on
the jaw........She fell.......and vas unconscious........I
vas going to take her upstairs and kill her there.....
But I am old........I sat in my apartment.....vatching
her.......hating her.......Then I heard a noise........It
vas your friend, very drunk........He passed out in
his doorvay..........so I helped him to bed...........then
I dragged her body to his bathtub............It took
a long time..............I slit her vrists..............so it
vould.........look like...........suicide...............then I
left her to die...................."

The heart monitor started to buzz. The lights
flashed wildly. The doctor waved JB away.

He stood back for a moment. When he left the
room he found Toby still waiting. Lieutenant Kelly
was with him.

"You heard?"

"Yes, Bent, I heard. Your friend is no longer a
suspect."

"Where is Len? He should be here to hear
this."

Toby said, "I went to his place before I came
here. But he wasn't there."

"Great. I solve one mystery for him and now he
provides a new one."

Kelly pulled out his notebook from his pocket.
"Before you go running off to solve that case I still
have a couple of questions about this one. How did
Mrs. Lucan get that bump on the back of her head if
she was unconscious?"

"Either when she fell in the Professor's apartment or she came to after he had cut her wrists. She could have stood up to get out of the tub but was too weak. That also explains how there was blood all over the bathroom. She probably passed out and banged her head again when she fell back into the tub."

Toby asked, "What's going to happen to the Professor now?"

Kelly said, "Nothing. The doctors don't expect her to live through the night. Her heart is too weak. She went too many years without getting any kind of medical care. This case is closed." He walked away.

"Well, the Professor almost got her wish," JB said.

"What was that?"

"To keep her secret until death. But in the process it included murder and the exposure of ten people's private lives. It's just like I've always thought.Secret's don't belong in closets anymore than people do."

Epilogue

The sixty or so people milled around the hall. They talked with each other, drank coffee, and found themselves places to sit. JB sat at the back of the room with a thoughtful expression on his face.

It had been an eventful few months since Mrs. Lucan and Professor VonWettering had both died.

JB moved to the East Side. Into Kenny and Blondel's old apartment in Toby's building. It was easy to open up the sealed door into Toby's place so they had a large space to share. On one of the walls now hung a small Toulouse-Lautrec sketch, bought from Helmut Lucan after being authenticated by an expert. The fraud case against Lucan had fallen apart when there were no witnesses who would admit they had purchased a fake from him.

The two boys, Kenny and Blondel, ended up where they belonged. Serving five to ten in an upstate prison. They had found a new apartment fast enough. What they hadn't counted on was the new landlady had lost a son to drugs. She turned them into the cops tout de suite.

Willie Hackshaw went back to the slammer. He's become very popular in prison theatricals since he now bares a striking resemblance to Al Pacino.

Toby's father, being investigated by both the government and the NYPD, decided it was too hot here in the USA and has retired to a villa outside Palermo. He's raising tomatoes as a hobby. The ownership of the apartment building was turned over to Toby.

Johnny Huge had retired from the porn business after his graduation from Visual Arts. He's now working as John Terillo, a director of commercials for a New York ad agency. What he had observed from in front of the camera he's now put to good use behind it. His style is considered suggestive and sexy.

Stormy Daze, after admitting to her past and now working at dropping hundreds of pounds, has found a new life as a media darling. Between TV appearances she's writing her memoirs. Len suggested she name them *Any Stripper Can Strip...But I Can Peal.*

Andrew Whitlow had decided to return to his wife and, as a result, became the *Daily News* scandal du jour. It turned out that Mrs. Whitlow knew of his dalliance with Jennifer. It was the latest in a long history of affairs during their marriage. What made this one different was it was the last one Mrs. Whitlow was going to stand for. Divorce papers that would have taken every possession Andrew Whitlow owned soon followed. Seeing his nice structured life crumbling around him sent Andrew a little around the proverbial bend. He became his ex-wives proverbial stalker.

His position at the Mayor's office disappeared when Mrs. Whitlow's restraining order against him became common knowledge. That simply gave him more time to pursue his ex-wife. One night, in the grip of his obsession, he staked out her house and frightened her so badly she grabbed a gun she had purchased to protect herself and shot out the living room window at the sounds she was hearing. Andrew Whitlow lay dead in the shrubbery. Mrs. Whitlow has been charged with manslaughter

Jennifer has left New York and ended up in Texas where she's snagged herself a rich oilman. She's living in luxury in Dallas.

JB was having his latest novel published. The original story had been replaced by a murder mystery about a blackout drinker who found a woman's body in his bathtub one morning. Also there was a play that was currently in rehearsals for an Off-Broadway run. Its story was about an older private detective and his young protégé working on the murder case of a young boy.

Toby happened to be perfect for the part of the protégé. JB hadn't exactly got him the part. He simply introduced Toby to the director.

Len got the part of the older detective by outright begging for an audition. He had to talk very hard to convince the director to trust him.

The chairman's voice brought JB back to the present. He said welcome to the crowd and gave the usual opening. Then he said, "I'd like to introduce our speaker for tonight's meeting. Celebrating his ninety day anniversary. Len M."

The applause rose and fell. Len looked out over the faces, locked on to JB's, smiled, and said, "Hello. My name is Len....and I'm an alcoholic."

About the author:

Ken Lansdowne has lived in California, Nevada, New York City, New Mexico, and now lives in Denver Colorado.

Secrets Don't Belong In Closets, the beginning, is the first novel in *The Bent Mystery* series. The second is *A Murderous Ball of Fluff.* Third is *The Fairy Dust Killer.* Fourth is *Home Sweet HoMo.* Fifth is *Dance:Ten Murder:Maybe?.* Sixth is *A Mystery, Wrapped In A Mystery, Surrounded By A Mystery.* Seventh is *The Art Of Death,* and number eight is *Bathhouse Bloodbath!*

There is also a Gay themed Christmas novella: *Jacob Marley*

If you would like to get an automatic e-mail when the next book in the series is ready for release sign up at k.lansd@outlook.com. Simply put the word "LIST" in the subject line of your email. Your e-mail address will never be shared and you can unsubscribe at any time.

Word-of-mouth is crucial for any author to succeed. If you enjoyed the book please consider leaving an Amazon online review, even if it is only a line or two: it would make all the difference and would be very much appreciated. If you didn't like it I apologize for taking up your time: my purpose was only to entertain or give you a laugh or two.